Code:
Elephants on
the Moon

Jennifer Bohnhoff

DEDICATION

No author is an island. I dedicate this book to the many who proofread
and critiqued, cajoled and encouraged me, but especially to Becky H.,
Marian M.K.., Chris E., Jean W., Noah R. and Patrice L., and to my family,
who toured the places in which this book occurred
and listened patiently as the story grew within me.

My gratitude goes out to my son, Matt Bohnhoff,
who created the map that is in the beginning of this book.
His patient, artistic spirit has guided me through many adventures.
I am indebted to Fred L. and Barbara H., whose technical expertise
was invaluable in getting the map into the proper format for this book.

But especially, this book is dedicated to those
who embarked on that gray D-Day morning, and to those who
are still offering up their lives for our freedom.

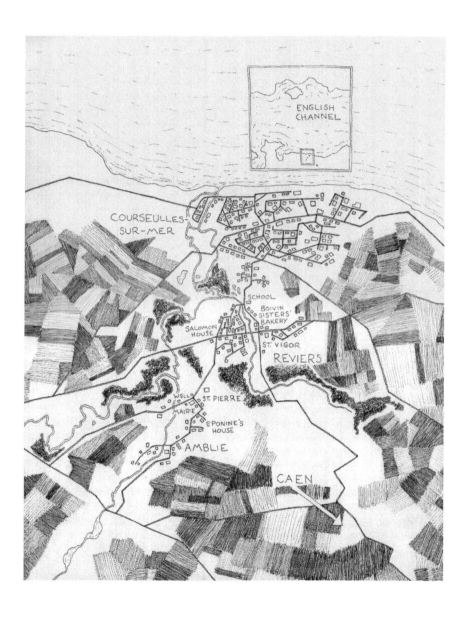

PROLOGUE
PARIS, FRANCE
AUGUST 1936

The little girl's mother hurled an old suitcase onto the unmade bed. Uneasy, the little girl distracted herself by moving to the apartment window. Traffic roared down the Rue Voltaire in a cacophony of honking horns and shouting voices. Two women passed, their faces hidden beneath broad brimmed hats. Their heels clicked against the pavement and their husky laughter filled the emptiness of the apartment. The little girl sighed. The city's rush and rumble comforted her.

Her mother sobbed and the little girl turned. She watched her mother jerk open a dresser drawer, pull out some clothes, wad them up and toss them into the open suitcase. The little girl clutched her toy pony tightly to her chest. Something about the way her mother's blood-red fingernails raked through the clothes frightened the child. She tugged at a strand of her carrot-red hair and sucked on it.

"Maman, where are you going?" she whined.

"Not me. Us. We must leave Paris."

"Why?"

Maman wiped her cheek with the back of her hand. She sobbed and slammed the suitcase shut, fiddling the latches closed. "It's something a six year old wouldn't understand." She crossed to the closet, got out another, smaller suitcase and filled it using the same desperate movements.

The little girl backed into the corner, wrinkling her crisp, blue satin dress. "Is Papa coming with us?"

Maman looked up, but she didn't look at her cowering daughter. Her eyes seemed unfocused and distant. "No. Your father is . . ." her voice trailed off in a choked whimper. The little girl pressed herself deeper into the corner, willing herself into the permanency of the wall. The woman turned her eyes on her daughter. They were focused this time, with a determination that made the little girl squirm. "Your Papa is a good man. He has gone off to build bridges. We just have to find a little place in the country and wait for him to return."

1

The little girl squeezed her pony tighter, pressing on the panic in her stomach. "What if he can't find us?"

The woman crossed the room and knelt in front of the girl. "He will find us. He will." She shook the child so hard that the pony's sawdust-stuffed head bobbled back and forth. The girl whimpered. Her mother released her grip.

"You will like it in the country," the woman said in a voice lodged somewhere between comfort and panic. "It will be peaceful there. I will buy you a pony – a real pony – all your own. Would you like that?"

The girl nodded. She had ridden a pony once – one of several connected to a metal merry-go-round in Luxembourg Garden. She remembered the sun lighting the soft, downy fur on its cheek and the gentle grinding sound it made as it champed on its bit. Maman and Papa had waved each time she came around the circle.

"Can I name it all by myself? Can I name it Galopin?"

The woman smiled and nodded. "You can name it anything you want. You and I, we are going to have new names, too."

"Why?" the little girl asked.

The woman squeezed the girl's shoulders. The blood-red nails dug into the child's arms. "It's part of a game we are going to play. No one will know about the game. It will be our secret. Do you understand?"

The little girl didn't understand, but she knew she must please her mother or the nails might dig deeper. She nodded.

"Good," Maman said. "From now on, I will be Jacqueline Lambaol and you will be my daughter Eponine."

"I'm already your daughter," the little girl said.

The woman nodded. "Then that part, at least, will be easy."

CHAPTER ONE:
ENEMIES WITHIN, ENEMIES WITHOUT

NORMANDY, FRANCE
APRIL 1944

Eponine dug her heels into Galopin's flanks and the massive Breton horse lunged into a gallop. Her auburn hair whipped into her eyes, making tears stream out of their corners, but Eponine didn't mind. Galloping on Galopin on this narrow path through a field of sprouting wheat was an emotional release, an escape from the ostracism she felt in Amblie, the small village in this provincial Norman backwater that she and her mother had moved to when she was six. The locals, who traced their ancestry in the region back fifteen generations, treated Eponine and her mother like outsiders even now, eight years later. Worse than outsiders. Just thinking about it made the tears stream even harder.

The locals should be giving the Germans the cold shoulder. They were the real outsiders. Four years ago General Petain, the decrepit old World War I hero who was now the leader of the French government, had signed an armistice with that fascist dictator Hitler and the German army had moved right in. Petain remained in control of southeastern France, which was now called Vichy France. He claimed to be neutral, yet he collaborated with the invaders.

As if collaboration had given the French people any relief from the oppressive occupiers. Under German military rule all of the local men had been conscripted into forced labor. Farm animals had been requisitioned, the fancy word for stolen. Food was strictly rationed. Travel forbidden. Listening to the radio was a crime.

So how could Eponine's neighbors prefer the Germans to her and her mother? Why were so many of her Norman neighbors so tolerant of an occupying army which brought nothing but hunger and deprivation, yet intolerant of her red hair and freckles? The thought made Eponine so mad that she spat in a long defiant arc that splattered into the green leaves like an incoming mortar shell. Take that, Norman neighbors. Take that, German Army.

Galopin came through the high, hedge-topped embankment that divided the field from the gravel road that entered the neighboring town of Reviers. She wiped away her tears with the back of her hand and took a breath to steady her nerves. An SS Panzer division was stationed in Reviers. The SS, Hitler's special, black-clad military force, was known for being especially ruthless. Eponine knew from past encounters that the young soldiers who drove and maintained the panzers, the German tanks, were also lonely. She needed more than spit bombs to protect her from homesick young soldiers. She patted her pocket to make sure she hadn't lost the ration books she needed to buy food. If there was a God in heaven, let Him protect her from the Germans -- and the merchants of Reviers.

Galopin turned the corner and Eponine reined him in to study the two blond soldiers loitering in front of the Boivin Sisters' Bakery. They leaned close-eyed against the horse rail, their cheeks turning russet in the warmth of the April sun. She marveled at how angelic they looked until she noticed the death skull insignia on their short-brimmed field caps. These men weren't angels. They were war demons. Eponine shuddered.

Impatiently, Galopin pawed the ground with his massive hoof and snorted, rousing the soldiers. They fingered their rifles, then realized that she was just a local schoolgirl on her horse and relaxed.

"*Guten Tag.*" The taller of the two smiled, exposing brilliant white teeth.

Eponine averted her eyes. She slouched, trying to hide her breasts. She was petite, small for her fourteen years. Perhaps, she thought wildly, they would ignore her if they thought she was only a child.

"Pardon," she said, guiding Galopin toward the horse rail and hoping that the soldiers would move away from it.

The tall soldier grabbed the cheek strap of Galopin's bridle, setting the horse into an uneasy dance. He looked up at Eponine, his blue eyes sparkling. Eponine turned her face away, pressing her lips together so tightly that she felt the blood drain from them. Her heart slammed into her chest as if trying to free itself.

The other solider took hold of Galopin's other cheek strap. He cooed at the horse, stroking the curved bridge of Galopin's nose in a way that showed he was comfortable around horses.

"Please. Just let me get my bread and go," Eponine said. The soldiers chuckled and talked between themselves before asking her something in their inscrutable, guttural language. Clearly, they didn't understand French. She didn't dare use the few curt German commands or curse words that she had picked up. Eponine's neighbor, Madame Deletombe, had cursed the Germans when they took her horse and had been pistol-whipped for it.

"Halt," Eponine said. The German word felt thick and ugly on her tongue.

The taller German let go of Galopin. For a moment she thought the crisis was past. Then he slipped his hand up her skirt and pressed the bare skin of her thigh.

Eponine stiffened. The German's smile had turned wolfish. His gaze dropped from her face to her chest. She threw her arm across her breasts and pulled back on the reins, digging her heels into Galopin's flanks, but the shorter German held on, cooing in Galopin's ear. The tips of the tall soldier's fingers dug into Eponine's flesh. A suppressed scream welled up in her chest. She clamped her lips together, denying it exit, so it spilled out in silent tears. She dashed away the tears with the back of her hand.

A third German voice, curt and commanding, distracted the two soldiers long enough for Eponine to leap off Galopin, throw his lead rope over the horse rail and dash for the bakery. Once safely inside, she leaned against the closed door. She couldn't stop shaking.

"*Bonjour, mesdames.*" Eponine gave the expected greeting even though her heart still battered against her ribcage and her face felt flushed, her hands cold and wet. Six housewives turned and gave her a scalding look before going back to their business of standing in line. With so little food, the town's shops were only open for a few hours every morning and a few more in the late afternoon. There were always lines. On shaky legs, Eponine took her place in the back of the queue and waited her turn.

Marie and Marthe Boivin's heads popped over the top of the display case at exactly the same time. Eponine couldn't tell the one from the other. Each was tiny and gaunt, with unnaturally black hair pulled into a severe bun at the back of her head. One cocked her head, the way a raven does. Eponine felt the sharp assessment of her beady black eyes. She watched the nostrils of the woman's long, narrow nose flare in disapproval. Eponine averted her gaze, self-consciously shifting from one leg to the other.

"Marthe," the sister said throatily, jerking her chin at Eponine.

The other nodded. "That foreign girl."

Exasperated, Eponine rolled her eyes heavenward. God, if He existed at all, hadn't heard Eponine's prayers. *"Pardon, Mesdames,* but you know I'm not foreign. I'm Breton." Eponine's mother said that auburn hair and hazel green eyes were common in Brittany. So was her first and last name. But to their Norman neighbors, the adjoining region of Brittany, which spoke a different language and had different music, customs and costumes, was as foreign as the moon.

"France for the French," one of the housewives added. "We should banish the Bretons to their Irish cousins."

The line of housewives murmured assent.

"We'd be better off if we did." Marie spat on the floor to emphasize her point.

With a gasp, Marthe grabbed the broom and spread the spittle around. "You mustn't let her provoke you that way."

Eponine leaned back on her heels and watched the two biddies peck at each other while Marie served their customers and Marthe spread the spittle into oblivion. Finally only she remained before the counter. Marthe threw the broom into a corner and thrust a bony hand over the counter, palm up.

"Your coupons, if you please. We haven't got all day."

Eponine fished in her pocket, then handed over three ration coupons and the cost of three loaves.

Marthe frowned at the coupons, stabbing at them with her finger. "Three loaves? Has your father come?"

"He's still building bridges," Eponine said, though in truth she wasn't sure. A lot of the men had been forced to work on Nazi construction crews. None had stayed away as long as her father.

"Then why three loaves?" Marthe pressed, though Eponine knew she knew the answer. Just like questions of her heritage, it was part of the goading game she was subjected to every time she entered the bakery. Marthe waggled her eyebrows up and down. "Ah yes! I remember! Your house guest, the very manly Madame Willocque."

6

Marie slapped three small, coarse loaves on the counter and glared at Eponine. "At least the mother doesn't fraternize with Germans, as her daughter does, right in front of our store."

Eponine thrust the bread into her string bag and left, slamming the door so hard that the windows rattled. It wasn't until the door was closed behind her that she remembered to look out for the Germans. Eponine took a hasty look around, but they were gone. She sucked in a deep breath and held it, then let it out in a slow whoosh. Her heart steadied. One more challenge, one more nasty word and she would have spoken her mind. The Boivins would have given her burned bread for the duration of the war, and the Germans would have pistol whipped her, but she didn't care. Her inability to resist grated on her more than German advances or village insolence. A hard ride on Galopin would quell her anger.

Eponine looked toward her horse, then froze, gawking at the tall, thin man who, half hidden behind Galopin's flank, held the lead rope. He was looking down the road so that Eponine only saw the right side of his face. Shiny red, burn-scarred skin stretched over the cheek. No nose flap covered his nostril and his ear looked like it had been whittled down to a nub. Eponine's heart leaped in hope. How many faces could be as damaged as that?

"Papa?"

The man turned his steel gray eyes to her and Eponine's heart leaped off the cliff of hope and plunged into desolation. This man wasn't her father. Her father's eyes were green, like hers.

The man moved around Galopin, revealing the field gray uniform of the Wehrmacht, the regular German army. The insignia on his sleeve showed that he was a sergeant. She averted her eyes, trying to avoid this German as she had the other two.

He clicked his heels in a quick, formal bow, then self-consciously turned his face, revealing a left side lined with wrinkles but undamaged by war. "I'm sorry if my appearance frightens you."

Eponine first recognized the voice that had distracted the other two soldiers, then noticed something even more startling. His speech was flawless. It held none of the guttural harshness of his fellow soldiers. She gasped. "You speak French?"

"I was raised near the border. As a boy I vacationed in Alsace. I love this country as much as my own."

Eponine frowned at his uniform. "Then leave us alone."

"Would that I could." He laughed bitterly. "And would that I could make those two SS ruffians leave you alone as well. Here. I shall teach you to tie a quick-release knot. If you drape the rope over the railing your horse might wander off."

"Not Galopin," Eponine said.

7

"Still, allow me to teach you." The man moved to Eponine's side, but she jerked the rope from him and in one smooth movement threw her leg over Galopin's back. Eponine cantered out of town without a backward glance, but her heart was in turmoil. If the French treated her badly and a German treated her with kindness, how could she know who was an enemy and who was a friend?

CHAPTER TWO
A FRIEND

Rocks shot from Galopin's massive hooves as he galloped toward Amblie. He slowed when he reached the break in the *bocage*. The shortcut through the wheat field lay on the other side of the break, but Eponine urged him on. The sunken road, hedged in by the bocage and shaded by tall trees, matched her mood. She felt too angry to savor the warmth of the sun on her face, her mind too clouded to face the broad expanse of open sky.

Why had her mother moved to Amblie? No one in Paris had cared that Eponine was Breton. She remembered her parents telling her how all of Paris had admired an African-American actress and singer named Josephine Baker in the 1920s, back before Eponine was born. Eponine snorted. What would the Boivin sisters do if dark-as-midnight Josephine Baker had moved to town instead of Jacqueline Lambaol and her red-headed daughter Eponine?

But Eponine's mother said things were different now that the Germans were in control, even in Paris. In Paris, like Berlin, Jews and other minorities disappeared. Some said they went east, to relocation camps in Poland. Others said to work camps. No one knew for certain. But that was no excuse for Maman to leave Paris. After all, it happened here in Normandy, too. Her one Jewish classmate, Sarah Salomon, had been in class one day. The next, the entire family had simply disappeared. No one cared. The villagers, busy peering into their empty soup pots, seemed to think that getting rid of the Jews might mean more food for the rest of them.

The road rose to a bald crest, where Eponine stopped and surveyed the countryside. Cabbage and lettuce, beans and the brilliant green of newly emerged wheat filled the undulating plain. Four miles to the north the Atlantic Ocean formed a thin, gray line along the horizon. Eponine closed her eyes and turned her face to the sun. Red and yellow patterns danced across her eyelids. She opened her eyes and stared at the distant sea. Blue sun spots burned into her vision appeared to float on the water like Allied battleships. Eponine sighed. If the Allies landed, the Germans would be forced to go away. Maybe the Allies would get rid of the Boivin sisters, too.

Eponine touched her heels into Galopin's flanks and the horse moved down the slope into the valley which hid Amblie. The way became dark, the air heavy with moisture. Massive tree branches blocked the sun's light and warmth. Something rustled in the tangle of undergrowth, making Galopin skittish. Eponine patted his neck.

"Hush," she said to him. Looking into the brush, she asked *"Ça va?"* If the answer came back in French or not at all, she thought she would be safe. If the answer was in German, it might be different. Either way, she couldn't bolt or she risked a bullet in her back.

"Ça va," a voice said, and then a young man parted the brush and stepped onto the road, adjusting the beret that the bushes had pulled askew. Eponine relaxed. She didn't recognize his dirt-smeared face, but not all the men hiding in the woods were from Amblie or Reviers. Though the man's clothes were a dingy gray, his face glowed with the joy of life. His eyes caught sight of Eponine's string bag and he smiled.

Eponine's stomach clenched. A hungry stomach did not discriminate between a German or a Frenchman; anyone who took its bread was cruel. But if her stomach didn't distinguish between a German soldier and a maquisard, a freedom fighter who used guerrilla tactics to harass the Germans, her head did. A maquisard was a hero of the people; surely he would not take bread from a hungry child.

"How are our brave maquisards?" Eponine asked

The man shrugged, pulling the strap of his rifle higher on his shoulder. "My comrades and I would rather stay in the bushes than perform forced labor in a German weapons factory, but we are cold and hungry. What have you got there?"

Eponine's clutched the bag to her chest. "Remember when loaves were big enough to really fill a person's stomach?"

"Remember when the French were patriotic enough to feed their soldiers?" The maquisard held out a hand, palm up.

Eponine considered galloping away, but the rifle on his shoulder stopped her. "Please. We are so hungry."

"You country people can afford to be generous with your fighters. You have gardens and livestock. In Paris, where I'm from, people eat crows, dogs and cats."

Eponine handed him one loaf. The maquisard made a disapproving clucking noise with his tongue. He put his hand exactly where the German had and squeezed. "You don't want me to force you, do you?"

Eponine winced. She handed over the bag. "You are as bad as the Germans, stealing our food."

"Not stealing. Requisitioning. But I tell you what; I will leave your family one loaf and my comrades and I will make do with just two. See? We are better than the German pigs. They want to take the whole country." He handed back the string bag, gave Eponine a rather lewd wink then disappeared into the brush. Eponine goaded Galopin toward home. She brushed back hot tears, angry at the thievery.

The road emerged into sunshine just as Eponine entered the cross roads that marked the beginning of Amblie. On her left lay a hill, into which steep stone steps, jumbled by centuries of frosts and thaws, climbed to the village church of Saint Pierre. Eponine's house was the first building up the road which passed in front of those steps. Directly in front of her the village's beehive-shaped well stood in the center of the village square. Beyond the square lay the Mairie, the building which was both the mayor's house and the town offices. So many German flags and buntings festooned the Mairie that Eponine's mother said it looked like a Nazi wedding cake.

A window on the second floor opened and René Bonté, the mayor's son leaned out so far that Eponine's heart quaked. René was far more handsome than those German soldiers, with straight dark hair and eyes so black it was hard for Eponine to tell where the pupils ended and the irises began. The village girls admired his looks. Their mothers admired his connections. But Eponine appreciated that he had been the only person, with the exception of Sarah Salomon, who befriended her.

"*Bonjour, ma petite roussette.*" René used the nickname that only he could, for she knew that he didn't hold her red hair against her. "I wish I could have ridden with you, but Papa says I can't ride Hortense now. Not without risking her foal. It will bring a very fine price when it's born. You went to market?"

Eponine bobbed in the best imitation of a curtsy that she could make on Galopin's back. She held up her string bag.

René raised an eyebrow. "A single loaf? Were the sisters out of bread again?"

"I bought three," Eponine said, "A maquisard took two from me on the way home."

"Those maquisards are riffraff and scoundrels." René shook his head in disgust. "They blow up the train tracks so the government can't bring food to the starving people, and when they slip away, who suffers?"

"Who, René?"

"Innocent villagers, that's who. Shot in reprisals because the cowardly maquisards won't stand and fight like men."

Eponine shifted uneasily on Galopin's back. "Aren't they fighting for France?"

René's older brother Jacques jostled his way into the window next to René. He wore the khaki shirt, black tie and beret that showed he was a member of the French Militia, which cooperated with the Germans to keep law and order in France. "Fighting for the fun of it, more like. The maquis pillage our farms and rape our women -- and take bread from innocent children. We members of the Militia are fighting for France, not those brigands." He peered at her, his eyes sharp and hungry. "Where were they?"

Eponine felt a stab of indecision, but the memory of the man's hand on her thigh and the groan of her hungry belly overrode her hesitance. Eponine pointed over her shoulder to the shaded lane and Jacques disappeared from view. Regret made Eponine cringe. There was something about one Frenchman hunting down another that seemed very wrong. She shook her head. "One can't trust anyone anymore."

René wagged his finger at her like a schoolteacher. "You should trust our allies the Germans. They would protect you."

"Protect me?" Eponine flushed as she remembered her encounter with the SS men in front of the bakery.

"*Mais oui!* Papa says that if it weren't for the Germans, the English would take our land, just as they did in the Hundred Years War. And the Americans would ruin our economy and the Soviets enslave us with evil communism."

Eponine giggled. Surely he had to be joking. This praise. All those German flags and buntings. Were they part of a carefully orchestrated plan to keep the Germans from confiscating the mayor's house and position? "As if the Germans haven't taken our land."

"Papa says that the German are only occupying our land until the threat is over," René said. "As soon as the Americans, British and Soviets are defeated, Hitler will give France back to the French."

Eponine tilted her head and smiled. "Do you believe everything your Papa says?"

"But of course! He is the mayor!"

Eponine decided to go along with the joke. She waved her arm as if she were waving the French Tricolor. "Liberty, Equality, Fraternity restored."

René looked shocked. "Our noble *Maréchal de France*, Philippe Pétain, will never let us go back to our corrupt republican ways. We must rally around our new motto: Work, Family, Country."

Eponine threw back her head and laughed. "*Vive la France*, René, and have a good supper."

"And the same to you, *ma petite roussette*. Perhaps we stroll together around the village after supper, since we cannot ride?"

"It would be my honor." Eponine turned Galopin up her own road. She liked how jovial René remained while everyone else either worried over food and firewood or harassed her. They had taken many pleasant rides before Hortense, the Bonté's magnificent black Arabian mare, became pregnant. She missed that time in the open air, the two horses nickering companionably to each other. Surrounded by enemies, there was one thing that Eponine could depend on, and that was René's friendship.

CHAPTER THREE
THE TRUTH

Eponine led Galopin into his stall in the empty cowshed and then, as she did morning and night, trudged back down the road to fetch water from the village's beehive well. Her buckets swung from the shoulder yoke, pendulums marking time in this wretched, primitive village. Their Paris apartment had its own bathroom, hot and cold running water, and a warm, gurgling radiator. Here there was no running water, hot or cold, and only an outhouse with a pit toilet.

Eponine filled Galopin's trough with half of one bucket before she picked up her string bag and took it and the rest of the water into the house. She was still chuckling over René's comments when she saw her mother and her father's cousin, Madame Willocque hunched over the kitchen table, deep in conversation. Memories of the Boivin sister's comments evaporated Eponine's levity.

They made an unlikely pair. Maman's hands and eyes made quick, darting movements like a sparrow after a grain of wheat. She always twisted her dark brown hair up in an elegant knot, and dressed her petite frame as if she worked in a fancy Parisian office. She looked chic, even when she worked in the fields or, until the Nazis had taken them, milked the cows. Barbe Willocque, on the other hand, was a stoop shouldered, hulking, raw-boned woman, with hair cropped so short that it stood out from her head like hedgehog spines. Her faded trousers and a stretched-out sweater made her look like a giant scarecrow. The Boivin Sisters were right. She did look manly.

"What is so funny?" Maman asked.

Eponine carefully slipped out of the yoke and poured her water into the large jar that sat on the kitchen counter.

"René was joking about how wonderful the Germans are for protecting us from English and Americans."

"The son of *Monsieur le Maire* isn't joking," Maman said.

"Of course he is. No one could really believe that rubbish." Eponine bent down and patted Madame Willocque's white terrier, Pétain. He looked up at her with rheumy eyes and then sneezed, bouncing on stiff legs. He looked just as ancient as his namesake, the World War One hero who now headed what remained of the French government in the south.

"The Pétainists believe it," Maman said. "*Maréchal Pétain* practically gave France to the Nazis because he thought the Germans would restore morality and order. *Monsieur le Maire* is one of their greatest supporters. Don't talk to his son anymore."

Eponine slammed the string bag onto the table and dropped heavily into her chair, throwing her hands up in a desperate gesture. "Now that Sarah is gone, René is the only pleasant person in all Normandy. Why can't we just go back to Paris?" She watched her mother and Madame Willocque study each other across the table, jaws clenching and unclenching. Each nodded her head almost imperceptibly. Eponine hated how these secret, wordless conversations made her feel like an outsider in her own home. Finally Maman nodded and Madame Willocque turned her dark eyes on Eponine, who felt the hair on the back of her neck stand up under the intensity of the gaze.

"Go ahead. Talk with René. Joke. Have fun. Pretend that you agree with his silly ideas. But be very careful what you say to him."

Maman snatched at the string bag. "Where is our meat?"

Eponine smacked her forehead with her palm. "I forgot to go to the *boucherie*."

Maman glared at her. "We can't afford to forget. I suppose you didn't argue when the Boivins shorted you on bread?"

"They didn't short me," Eponine said. "A maquisard stole two loaves. But I told Jacques where to find him. The Militia will bring him to justice."

Maman and Madame Willocque sprang to their feet. They stared at each other for a moment, a second silent conversation passing between them over the table.

"Do you think . . .?" Maman asked.

Madame Willocque nodded. "You'd better."

Maman thrust out her hand. "Give me the coupons – quickly! I will go for the meat. I will have to rush if I'm to have dinner on the table before the electricity goes off."

"It doesn't always go off at six," said Eponine. "Sometimes it doesn't go off at all."

"Who wants to chance it?" Muttering under her breath, Maman threw on her sweater. She kicked off her house slippers, slammed her feet into her clogs, and stormed out the door.

"She doesn't have to be so snitty about it," Eponine said.

"Don't you realize what you've done?" Barbe Willocque nearly shouted the words. She stood there for a moment, clenching and unclenching her fists, then she burst into one of her frequent coughing fits. Eponine was afraid Madame Willocque's lungs would spurt out of her mouth. Finally Madame dropped listlessly into a chair and let out a sigh. She seemed to deflate. "Jacqueline is just trying to keep us healthy. You really need the meat."

Eponine slumped even farther in her chair. "I didn't just forget. Two soldiers made advances, then the Boivins were terrible, and an old sergeant who looked like Papa tried to talk to me. It was too much."

Eponine picked a fork off the table and twirled it between her fingers. She set it down hastily, fighting the urge to plunge it into the tabletop. "God! I hate this war. I hate this place. I miss Papa. And there's nothing I can do to fix any of it."

"You can start by not taking the Lord's name in vain." Madame Willocque's glare was so intense that Eponine had to look away.

"It's just an expression. It doesn't mean anything. I don't even believe in God."

They sat there, the one glaring and the other staring at the table, the ground, the dog, anywhere but Madame Willocque's face until Eponine could take the silence no longer. "How can we all just sit and let the Nazis run our lives?"

"We aren't just sitting," Madame Willocque said, "and there is plenty you can do. Refuse to talk to the Germans. Keep up your spirits and your health. Eat as well as the ration cards will allow. Study hard in school. Your time will come, and you have to be educated and ready to act."

Eponine slouched even lower. She had the sudden desire to punish this woman for offering no sympathy. "Do you know what the Boivin sisters call you? Madame Monsieur. They think you and Maman are lovers."

Barbe Willocque sat poker straight, her face flushed crimson. "Children shouldn't think about such things."

Eponine shrugged. "They talk about it in the schoolyard. They say that, with all the men gone, women turn to other women for comfort."

Madame Willocque snorted. "Some women, maybe. Ah, well. Let them think what they will. It will blind them to other possibilities."

"What other possibilities?" Eponine sat a little straighter.

Madame ran her hand through her hair, making it stand on end. The sinews on the back of her hand stood out like ropes. She had gained weight since she had arrived very early one cold February morning, but she was still terribly thin. She stared at her short, split fingernails. Her cuticles were dry and jagged. "I'm not trying to look like a man."

"I know," Eponine said. "The doctors cut your hair to save you."

"That is the story," Barbe Willocque said.

A scuffling sound overhead made both women look up. Eponine pointed. "There it is again. We have mice in the attic."

Barbe Willocque sighed. "Next time a maquisard demands your food, tell him that Ursule says to leave you alone."

"Ursule? Who is Ursule?"

Madame Willocque pushed herself heavily away from the table. "Never mind. Go curry that mangy old horse of yours while I deal with the mice."

Eponine slammed the door behind her and stomped to the cow barn. "You aren't mangy," she muttered as she brushed the knots out of Galopin's tail. Galopin brought his ears forward as if he were really listening. "Old, yes, but you can still plow a field and canter to town. Hortense may gallop faster, but she can't pull a plow. And you aren't as handsome and lithe as she is, but Bretons are bred for strength, not beauty. Us Bretons must stick together."

The Nazis hadn't confiscated Galopin because they wanted the cabbages and peas he carted to town more than they wanted an odd, old horse, so it was good that he was who he was. And it was good that the Bontés were who they were as well, or the beautiful Hortense would have been taken away long ago, just like the neighborhood's cows and horses. Being *Monsieur le Maire* had its privileges.

Eponine brushed Galopin's broad, stubby body and his short, stocky legs. She threw her arms around his massive neck and giggled, remembering how René had teased her last summer when the two of them stopped riding to let their horses drink from a stream. Don't get off his back, he cautioned. If you do, the weight of his head is going to bring his back legs off the ground. That René. Always making jokes.

Or was he? Did he really believe the silly political statements he'd spouted that afternoon?

Eponine stared into the distance, remembering the long, meaningful look that had passed between Maman and Madame Willocque. Did their secrets concern Papa? Did they explain why she and her mother moved to this narrow minded village? That is the story, Madame Willocque had said when Eponine brought up the illness that caused her short hair.

The word story echoed in Eponine's mind. Did it mean that Madame hadn't really been ill? Why, then, was she so thin, her hair so short, her skin and fingernails weak and cracking?

How much of what Eponine believed to be truth was really just pretense and story?

Galopin nipped Eponine's shoulder. It wasn't enough to hurt, but it brought Eponine back to the present. "I'm sorry," she said as she brushed him, "but things aren't as they seem. And tonight, at dinner, I intend to learn the truth."

CHAPTER FOUR
THE CRUELEST MONTH

Eponine jolted awake to find Barbe Willocque shaking her. She jerked her shoulder away and sat up. Her face felt flushed where it had pressed into the school books scattered across the kitchen table. She wiped drool from her composition tablet and rubbed sleep from her eyes, then put away her books.

"I never used to doze off over my studies," she grumbled.

Maman set three steaming bowls on the table. "The headmaster, Monsieur Couturier says many of his students fall asleep these days. He says the doctor calls it 'hunger sleepiness.'"

The full-bodied, salty scent of potatoes and meat, carrots and onions made Eponine's mouth water. She looked at the bowl and realized that her nose had tricked her. The soup was only a thin broth with a few shreds of meat and vegetable floating in it.

Maman set a bowl in the center of the table. "I made a salad of the dandelion greens that are sprouting along the edges of the fields now. My mother used to say they were a good spring tonic." She added a basket of thinly sliced bread and a pot of ersatz jam made from concentrated grape sugar.

Ersatz, the German word for fake, described most everything these days. There was ersatz coffee, ersatz tobacco, ersatz sugar made from saccharine, even a nasty, oily substance called ersatz butter. Eponine shuddered. The whole world seemed fake.

A sliver of carrot floated listlessly in her soup. The fact that it wasn't ersatz didn't raise her spirits. Now that spring promised abundance, the food seemed even skimpier. She wiped back a tear.

Madame Willocque cleared her throat with a deep, hacking, disconcerting cough and began reciting in English, translating into French at the end of each phrase so that Eponine and her mother could understand:

"April is the cruelest month, breeding
Lilacs out of the dead land, mixing
Memory and desire, stirring
Dull roots with spring rain.

Winter kept us warm, covering
Earth in forgetful snow, feeding
A little life with dried tubers."

Eponine stirred her soup. The limp carrot slice swirled like an autumn leaf. "I thought that maquisard was on my side."

"There are good and bad people on both sides," Madame said. "Trust one and fight the other, regardless of whose side they are on."

"How can you tell who is good and who is bad?"

"Ah, now that is the real question."

"Eat your soup," Maman stabbed her finger towards Eponine's bowl.

Eponine picked up her spoon, but questions swirled about her mind. "Who wrote that poem?"

"An Englishman named T. S. Elliot. It's from a poem entitled 'The Wasteland.' Appropriate, no?"

"How come you know it?"

"I taught English literature at the Sorbonne before the war."

"I bet your English would be useful in the Résistance. You could communicate with the allies who help our maquisards."

Maman thrust the bread basket towards Eponine. "Stop talking. Eat."

Out of the corner of her eye, Eponine watched her mother shred a piece of bread into tiny crumbs. Eponine didn't know what she was searching for, but her mother's reaction told her that she was getting close to some truth which had been withheld from her.

"The Résistance would find me of little use," Madame said. "My English is scholarly. I read it, but I don't speak it well."

"You weren't sick, were you? You didn't lose your hair because of illness."

Maman leaped from the table and in a frenetic burst of energy collected cups from the shelf and the coffee pot from the stove. "Coffee, anyone?"

"What do you think happened to my hair?" Madame Willocque asked.

"I don't know," Eponine admitted.

Maman hurriedly poured ersatz coffee, a thin, muddy concoction made from roasted barley that tasted like tree bark. She shoveled several spoonfuls of sticky, concentrated grape sugar into Eponine's cup. "Here! I've given you extra sugar. Drink up! Barbe, it's time you and I do the dishes."

Eponine grabbed Madame Willocque's wrist. The woman's dark, inscrutable eyes burned into hers. Their intensity made Eponine squirm, but she didn't back down. "I won't drink my coffee until I know the truth."

"Children have suffered worse deprivations than missing their coffee," the house guest answered.

Eponine sagged in defeat. "I can't stare you down. I can't intimidate you. There isn't anything left for me to do but beg. Tell me, *s'il vous plait.*"

"Very well." Barbe Willocque stretched her legs out in front of her. "It's as you say. I wasn't sick. Society was. I was imprisoned in Royallieu Camp, near Compiègne. Later, I was sent to Ravensbruck, near Berlin. But I escaped."

"Prison? For what?" Eponine asked.

"Enough," Maman gasped.

Eponine shivered. "Aren't you afraid someone will report you to the Gestapo?" One was better dead than in the hands of the Gestapo the henchmen of Hitler's intelligence system.

"Everyone in Amblie and Reviers knows that I, your father's distant cousin Barbe Willocque, came to the country to recover from tuberculosis. My identity papers prove it. The Gestapo checked my papers when I came and found everything in order."

"Why didn't you tell me this before?" Eponine remembered the terrifying roar of the Citroen's engine as it came down the hill into Amblie. Whenever Eponine heard a smooth running engine, she assumed there was a German behind the wheel. The Germans had confiscated almost all oil and gasoline, so French vehicles burned wood in smoky, temperamental *gasogene* engines which made a racket that one could hear for miles.

"The more you know, the more danger you are in," Madame said.

"No more questions!" Maman whined.

Eponine put up a hand to stop her mother. "One more. How did an old dog like Pétain survive the work camps?"

Barbe Willocque chuckled. "I found him wandering the lanes just two days before I arrived on your doorstep. Though he was starving, the little dog persisted in thinking himself very grand and important indeed. Instantly I knew I must keep him and I knew what he should be named."

"I thought you'd had him since he was a pup," Eponine said.

"That, too, is part of the story," Madame Willocque said. "Just as you think that I'm . . . "

"Enough!" Maman leaped away from the table. She pulled a few cans and packages from the nearly empty shelves and tossed them into a market basket with clattering speed, then thrust the basket into Eponine's hands.

"Here," Maman said, "Be useful. Take these to Father Simon. I think he is up at the church. Tell him it's another package for our poor, starving cousins in Paris."

Nearly every week Eponine delivered foodstuffs to Father Simon, who packaged them properly and sent them on their way – at least, that was the story. She had never before questioned for whom they were intended, but now Eponine thought back to her Parisian life. It was a long time ago and she had been quite young, but she was sure she had never met any cousins.

"We're not feeding those thieving maquisards, are we?" Eponine asked. "Is that why we moved to Amblie? To support maquisards?"

The anger in her tone upset Pétain, who hopped around on stiff legs, barking his thin, dry bark.

Maman's hands fluttered like two wounded birds. For a moment Eponine thought her mother was going to tell her the truth. But then Maman dropped into a chair and put her face in her hands. Eponine silently pulled the door shut behind her, her mother's miserable sobs stabbing her heart. For a split second she regretted asking so much of her mother, but then the pain passed, replaced by a surge of annoyance. It wasn't her fault she didn't know where her father was or who Madame Willocque was or why they lived in Amblie. Eponine squared her shoulders and stepped determinedly toward the church. If Jacqueline Lambaol wouldn't tell her the truth, she would learn it from Father Simon.

A figure emerged from the shadows. Eponine shrieked and leaped back, slamming herself into the wall and knocking all the wind from her lungs. She gasped, both because of the collision with the wall and confusion. The world had shifted under her feet and everything Eponine assumed to be true was now in question. She put a hand to her thundering heart.

René Bonté stuck out his lower lip and batted his black lashes at Eponine. "I've been waiting for nearly a quarter hour. Did *ma petite roussette* forget that she promised to stroll with me after supper?"

"I can't walk with you. I must run an errand for Maman. Goodbye." Eponine set out briskly.

René jogged to keep up with her. "Where?"

"To Father Simon." She held up the basket, as if it explained everything.

"Charity is good for the soul! But the rectory is that way." René pointed the other direction, toward the tiny house where the priest and his housekeeper, the Widow Tournebulle lived. It was an act of true Christian charity to allow Widow Tournebulle to keep her situation. She was a slovenly housekeeper and a worse cook and the Boivin sisters claimed she hadn't bathed since her husband died during the Great War. But all the gossips in the village knew she couldn't tell the priest's business since she was deaf as a stump. She was twice as stout as a stump, too. A handsome young priest might be tempted into sin by a younger, more beautiful or more competent housekeeper.

"I'm not going to the rectory. I'm going to the church," Eponine said.

René clapped his hands together like a delighted child. "You should confess something while you are there. Papa says confession is good for the soul. He says the whole nation must confess and then purge ourselves of Socialists, Jews, Freemasons, Communists, Jazz Musicians. Then we will rise to our former glory."

Eponine stared at the mayor's son. His words weren't funny anymore. The image of Sarah Salomon's empty house loomed in her mind. How empty the entire country would be if René Bonté and his father had their way.

"Just them? We get rid of them and France will be saved?"

René shrugged. "Well, I suppose I left someone out. Did I mention the trade unionists? Civil libertarians? Oh, yes! And the gypsies! We can't forget them."

They had come to the bottom of the stone stairs that led to Saint Pierre's. Eponine jerked her chin toward the Mairie. "I will see you tomorrow."

"No, *ma petite rousette*. It would be my honor to accompany you." He hooked his elbow in Eponine's and turned her around, escorting her up the stairs in what he must have thought very chivalrous fashion.

They found Father Simon bent over in the graveyard that surrounded the church, pulling weeds in the last few minutes before twilight made work impossible. He groaned as he straightened up, a hand on the small of his back.

"Ah, Eponine, René. I'm too young to feel this decrepit."

Eponine studied the unwrinkled face of the priest and smiled into the melting, chocolate-colored eyes. If he weren't a priest, she would choose him to walk with in the evenings instead of the mayor's son.

"Backbreaking work is backbreaking, no matter your age, Father. Here. Maman wanted me to deliver these."

Father Simon took the basket. He peered solemnly into René's face, then Eponine's. Eponine thought he wanted to say something but didn't dare. "Yes, my child. I know exactly what to do with these. Now go quickly, with my blessings. It won't look seemly if the mayor's son was caught out after curfew with a girl."

René slapped a palm to his forehead. "But of course! I must not besmirch our precious reputations." He grabbed Eponine's hand and dragged her pell mell down the stairs.

CHAPTER FIVE
ELEPHANTS ON THE MOON

No lights shone from the windows of Eponine's house. It looked deserted – as cold and dead as the Salomon house.

Eponine missed Sarah Salomon. She had been the only girl at school willing to befriend an outsider because she was an outsider, too. Sarah said that Jews were always outsiders wherever they lived. Eponine remembered going home with Sarah after school some days. She had watched Sarah touch the little metal box on the door frame and had asked her friend what it was. Sarah told her that all Jewish families had one, that it held portions of their Bible. Although she wasn't religious herself, Eponine had thought that a nice idea. Inside, Madame Salomon cooked while three daughters and one son buzzed about and Monsieur Salomon's sewing machine filled the rooms with its warm whirr. He was the best tailor in Reviers. Now that he was gone, Eponine's Maman had to go to the clothing shops in Cruelly, five miles to the west. But most of the time the shelves and racks in those stores sat empty.

Empty, as Eponine's house appeared to be. By German mandate, villagers hung heavy black blankets over their windows to prevent American and British bombers from using village lights to navigate. The blackout was supposed to protect them, just as the presence of the Panzer division in Reviers was supposed to protect them. Eponine wondered what wonderful benefits René would attribute to blackouts if he had the chance.

A pale sliver of light spilled into the yard as Eponine opened the door and stepped in. She pulled the door tight behind her. Madame Willocque sat in Papa's old chair. The wick on the kerosene lamp at her elbow burned low, barely above the clamp that held it. The electricity must be out again.

Madame Willocque turned her face to the clock that stood on the mantel over the cold fireplace just as it struck a single bong. Eight-thirty. "That took longer than I'd thought. Did you and Father Simon have a good talk?"

Eponine dragged a kitchen chair across the room and dropped onto it. "René Bonté followed me. I couldn't talk with him around."

Madame Willocque nodded. "That boy would blab your words to all the wrong people. He has a big mouth, but a little brain."

Eponine chuckled. "You've been here a few months and already know René better than I do."

"His beauty blinded you." She took a deep breath then let it out in a long, thin stream. "You must learn to look beneath the surface. Things and people aren't always what they seem."

Eponine leaned forward, resting her forearms on her knees. "Tell me about prison camp."

Madame Willocque shook her head. "It's too terrible to talk about."

"Can you at least tell me why you were there?"

"Because I'm Jehovah's Witness," Madame answered.

"What's that?"

Barbe Willocque winced, as if Eponine's question had struck her like a fist. "A religion, different from Catholicism or Judaism. There aren't many of us, and that makes us easy to persecute. And I was hiding Jews, another reason to arrest me."

She leaned back and sighed and the words she had said were too terrible to say came out. "There were hundreds of women at Royaillieu. They issued a bowl to each of us. We got half a liter of water a day, to wash and to drink. Sometimes we got gruel. Sometimes, bread. Never enough. The latrine was a ditch next to the fence that separated the women's section of the camp from the men's section. Men entertained themselves by watching women squat."

"Disgusting," Eponine said.

Madame Willocque nodded. "Your dignity is the first thing the Nazis try to wrest from you when they incarcerate you. You must be very strong."

She pointed to the left side of her chest, right over her heart. "They put a badge on each of us. Right here, so they could see it. Jews wore the same yellow stars they must to wear outside of camps. Communists wore red rectangles. And we Jehovah's Witnesses wore purple triangles. It was intended to isolate us, but I considered mine a badge of honor, worn near my heart. It gave me strength."

"Tell me about Ravensbrück," Eponine said.

Madame shook her head and pointed to the stairs. "I won't give you nightmares. Someday, when the sun is shining brightly and we don't worry about being sent away, I will tell you. For now, it's bedtime."

"I never had to go to bed this early before the war."

"You weren't starving then. You must conserve your energy so you won't fall asleep over your books. Now, go."

Eponine reluctantly dragged herself out of her chair and up the stairs to her bedroom. She wriggled into the ratty nightgown which she had worn for the past three years. It had gotten so small that she could barely bend her arms. Thoughts of her encounters with the SS men, the maimed Wehrmacht sergeant, the maquisard and the mayor's son flashed through her mind. How could she look beneath the surface? Tell reality from image? Good from evil? How could she distinguish friend from foe in a war where everyone seemed so sure that their side was right?

Eponine slipped between the cool sheets and stared into pitch blackness. Did stars twinkle outside the blanketed window? She had been too preoccupied with René to watch them emerge in the darkening sky. She rummaged under her pillow for her little stuffed pony. It was no more than a limp bit of rags which had lost most of its sawdust stuffing, but she found it comforting. Tonight she needed that comfort.

It struck Eponine that she didn't know her mother. Maman appeared fussy and nervous, too timid to face the Reviers shopkeepers. Could that kind of person shelter a prison camp refugee? There had to be more to her mother than Eponine thought.

Regardless of how strong Maman might be, Eponine had treated her badly by making her walk to Reviers in the stiff wooden clogs she had worn since her shoes had fallen to bits over the winter. Eponine's own shoes were patched with soles cut from a bald automobile tire, but at least they bent when she walked. Guilt prodded Eponine out of bed. She owed her mother an apology. Shivering from the cold damp, Eponine stuffed her feet into her worn slippers and crossed the hall to the room where her mother shared the double bed with her house guest. A pale moon cast blue light on the coverlet. Eponine felt the unease of confusion. Where were her mother and Barbe? Then, in a jolt of recognition, she realized that their window was uncovered. What was going on?

Eponine descended the steps in silence. The tick of the mantel clock boomed like rifle shots in the dark kitchen.

"Maman?" she whispered. "Madame Willocque?"

No one answered. Eponine took a breath to steady herself, then stepped into the darkened room. She bumped into a chair. The old terrier leaped to his feet in a fit of barking.

"Pétain? Here, boy," Madame Willocque's voice called, but Pétain didn't go to his mistress. He snorted, turned three times around, and collapsed in a snoring heap beneath the table.

Eponine's heart pounded in her ears. All was silent for a long while, then she heard a murmur of voices followed by a weird, elastic whine.

Eponine recognized the sound of a radio seeking the right frequency. It confused her. Only the Mayor was allowed to have a radio, so that he could distribute the official news and allow people to listen to sanctioned programming. Surely she wasn't hearing the mayor's radio all the way over here?

She tilted her head and determined the sound was coming from the stairs to the coal cellar that ran behind the fireplace.

Because the ground never froze solid or heaved with frost in Normandy, very few houses had cellars or basements. Eponine's house, however, had a tiny coal cellar no bigger than six feet by six feet, with a slanting door on the outside wall through which coal could be poured and a set of stairs behind the fireplace from which it could be retrieved. Before the war, Eponine stood on the bottom stair to shovel coal into her bucket, but the supply dwindled as the war continued. For quite some time now, Maman burned fallen branches from the forest in the fireplace and stove. The cellar remained a forgotten hollow, a dirt-floored cave with a few old barrels of rags and rubbish in the corner.

Eponine lifted her slippers one at a time, making slow, stealthy progress towards the fireplace. A faint light emanated up the stairs. Her mother and Barbe Willocque knelt in the dirt, their backs a black wall which hid both lantern and radio from Eponine's view, but she knew both were there. She knew because of the shadows cast on the ceiling and the faint, off-station whine. Maman wasn't listening to either Jean Hérold-Paquis or Philippe Henriot, the two Nazi sympathizers whose voices dominated the airwaves of Radio-Paris. What was she up to?

Eponine took a deep breath, then started down. The air grew cooler and damper with each step. The cold reached up under her nightgown, making the hairs on her shins stand on end. As she passed the chimney foundations, the clock on the mantel struck the hour.

Bong.

Bong.

Bong.

Bong.

Bong.

Bong.

Bong.

Bong.

Bong.

Nine o'clock. She took one more step. The stair groaned as it yielded to her weight. With a little shriek of panic, Eponine's mother stuffed the radio into the rag barrel while Barbe Willocque leaped to her feet. Her fists were poised at her sides like a prize fighter entering the ring. The terrible mixture of grim determination and anger on her face made Eponine want to flee. Madame Willocque moved and the light fell on Eponine, who shielded her eyes from its glare.

Madame Willocque relaxed. "It's you."

"Go back to bed," Maman's hands fluttered upwards as if fanning her daughter up the stairs.

Barbe Willocque put out a hand. "Too late for that now. Hush. We must listen."

Jacqueline Lambaol retrieved the radio from the barrel and set it on the floor. Four notes – the dot, dot, dot, dash that was the beginning of Beethoven's Fifth Symphony – came through the static. Eponine sucked in her breath. Children whispered in the schoolyard that this was the how the BBC, the British Broadcasting Company, began the Free French's nightly program. If the Gestapo knew they were listening to this, Madame Willocque, Jacqueline Lambaol and Eponine would all be shot as spies.

A voice on the radio spoke in French. "This is London; today, April 10, 1944, on the one thousand, three hundredth and ninety-fifth day of the French people's struggle for their liberation, the French speak to the French." He followed with summaries of the news that were very different from the ones given out by the Mayor. According to the BBC, the Germans weren't doing well at all. Eponine laughed, delighted with how different this news was from the official news she heard at school.

"Hush," Barbe Willocque hissed. "This is important."

"And now some special messages," the announcer said. "The siren has bleached hair. Electricity dates from the twentieth century. The moon is full of elephants."

"The moon is full of elephants?! What does that mean?" Eponine said.

Her mother glared at her. "To someone, it means a great deal."

Eponine dropped onto the dirt floor. She crossed her legs and her arms to ward off the chill and tried to make sense of the gibberish. Finally the strange messages ended and a song, Le Chant des Partisans, began.

Friend, do you hear the black flight of crows over our plains?
Do you hear the muffled cries of the country that is enchained?
Whistle, companions, in the night liberty listens to us.

Maman tucked the radio deep within the rags. "Well, now you know why we send you to bed so early. Go back to bed. Forget you saw this. It was a dream, no more."

Eponine shook her head. "This is no dream. You harbor a fugitive, deliver foodstuffs to the priest to feed the maquisards, listen to illegal broadcasts. Are you a member of the Résistance? Is that why we moved to Normandy?"

Maman shook her head. "Don't be silly. The food goes to our cousins in the city. And we moved here long before Hitler invaded, before the Résistance movement began. Now go to bed."

"Not until I know the truth." Eponine crossed her arms even more tightly over her chest.

Barbe Willocque sighed and ran her boney hand over her brow. "It's over, Jacqueline. You can't protect her any longer. She knows too much."

"I don't want her involved," Maman said.

"She already is," Madame said. "She delivers packages to Father Simon. It's time to give her bigger assignments."

Eponine hunched her shoulders, much as she had when the SS men confronted her in front of the bakery. "Keep me out of it. Just tell me where my Papa is."

"Weren't you just telling me this afternoon that you felt useless?" Madame Willocque asked.

"I don't want to be involved. It's dangerous. And illegal."

Barbe Willocque frowned. "And just what makes you think we do anything dangerous or illegal?"

"Elephants on the moon, Ursule."

Maman nodded at Madame Willocque. "You are right. She knows too much. We begin training her tomorrow."

CHAPTER SIX
COAL DUST

The next day at school Eponine squirmed at her desk. Members of the Résistance blew up bridges. They derailed trains and cut telephone and telegraph lines. She tried to envision herself crawling through a ditch, Nazis patrolling the ridge over her, but failed. She didn't think she had the inner strength to do what Madame Willocque expected.

Eponine set her hands on her desk. Her music teacher, Mademoiselle Pithou, said they were too small to play piano. Eponine made a ring out of her thumb and forefinger and placed it around her wrist. She stuck her leg into the aisle, studied her ankle and smiled ruefully. The boys called her bird legs for a reason. Her bones were tiny, like sparrow bones. She was the shortest in her class. Students two years younger towered over her. Eponine decided to tell Madame Willocque that she was too small and too young to do anything dangerous.

Anxious to get the encounter behind her, Eponine ran home at the end of school. She arrived breathless and flushed. The farmhouse was empty. She raced into the fields before she lost her resolve. There she found Madame Willocque and Maman bent nearly double as they planted tiny lettuce seeds in the yellow-brown soil.

"I'm here," Eponine said through her gasps. "Now, about my assignment. . . ."

Barbe Willocque started to speak, but a paroxysm of coughing overtook her. When it was over, she painfully straightened to her full height. Her hand on the small of her back, she grimaced at the high, thin clouds that scooted overhead. "First, calm down. You must look like you are doing nothing unusual, nothing out of your ordinary routine."

"I am calm," Eponine said, "but you must know that . . ."

A sharp glance from Maman silenced her. She took a deep breath and willed her racing heart to slow to normal.

"This is what I want you to do," Barbe said. "Take a metal bucket – not one of the milking pails, mind you. Go to the Salomon house. Go down to their coal cellar and scrape up the black dirt. We need coal dust."

Eponine's body tensed. "Are you going to set fire to Gestapo headquarters?"

"Of course not. We are going to cook supper." Maman reached into the pocket of her apron and brought out the ration books. "Here. While you are in town, you can get our bread from the Boivin Sisters."

Eponine felt loose and disjointed. This assignment wasn't dangerous. It seemed rather mundane. She breathed a sigh of relief and gathered the bucket and her string grocery bag, then rode Galopin into town. But even though her head told her this errand wasn't dangerous, her heart beat erratically. She told herself to calm down. This wasn't, as Madame had said, her first act of resistance. She had carried packages to Father Simon for some time. Eponine picked up the bread without incident and proceeded to the Salomon's house, one of the identical yellow stone houses that lined the main street so closely that passersby could easily peer into their lower windows when the shutters were opened. The Salomon's shutters hadn't been opened in some time. A German seal on the front door announced that the house and all its contents were now government property, but Eponine knew that there was little within the house. Soon after the family had disappeared, someone had broken the seal on the back door and stolen all the valuables. She guided Galopin up the alley.

The back door of the Salomon house hung on broken hinges. A drift of leaves, like golden snow, crunched under Eponine's feet as she entered. No pots or pans hung near the cold fireplace. The wood rack was empty, as were the cupboards. She called to make sure she was alone, then slipped into the coal cellar. Pale light filtered down the stairs. Eponine groped around for the flat-fronted shovel and started filling her bucket.

There was more coal dust here than in her own home – small chunks even, as large as road gravel. The pieces clattered into the metal bucket, filling the room with dust. She coughed.

Her bucket was half filled when a flashlight beam snapped on at the top of the stairs. Eponine froze, the shovel suspended over the bucket.

"What are you doing down there?" a voice asked.

Eponine relaxed at the sound of French. She held up the bucket. "Gathering coal dust," she answered, hoping he was a sympathetic neighbor.

"Well, my petite rider, you are stealing German coal dust."

Eponine shielded her eyes from the flashlight's glare and recognized the

Wehrmacht sergeant with the burned face. Eponine's mind raced through all the possibilities. She wanted to flee, but how? He was standing on the stairs, the only exit. She was trapped and obviously guilty of both stealing and trespassing. If he shot her on the spot, no one could protest. But this German had been kind to her once before. Perhaps he would be so again.

"Should I pour it back out?"

He chuckled. "Poor child. Reduced to stealing coal dust. I knew it was you when I saw that horse of yours in the kitchen yard. You're right. He doesn't wander, even if you don't tie him up. Like me, I think he is too old and tired to bother. Ah well, be off with you. *Raus.*"

"*Raus?*" she asked.

"It means hurry, before my patrol gets curious."

"Thank you, monsieur," Eponine's knees shook as she followed the sergeant's light up the stairs. She leaped onto Galopin's back and clattered down the cobblestone road, careful not to jog the bucket hard enough that black dust billowed from it. It was hard to ride slowly when her heart raced.

She rode into the yard and found her mother and Madame Willocque waiting. Maman, who had been wringing her hands, looked frantic with fear. She pulled Eponine off Galopin's back and crushed her in a desperate embrace.

"Were there any problems?" Maman said.

Eponine shook her head. "None at all." It was a lie, but her mother didn't need the terror of the truth. Not now, when the task was complete.

"You have done well," Barbe Willocque said, "but the job is only half done. After dinner we three will complete it."

Eponine's head whirled through dinner. She didn't dare ask what she must do next. She had stolen coal dust and nearly been shot for it. What more did they expect of her? The answer, it turned out, wasn't as terrible as she imagined. Her Maman showed her how to mix a thin paste from water and coal dust.

"Now we destroy evidence." Maman reached under the kitchen rug and pulled out a small sheaf of newspapers.

Eponine read the title and gasped. A person could get in a lot of trouble for having a copy of the underground newspaper Combat in her house. "How long has that been there?" she asked.

"Too long for my comfort," Maman answered. "I was afraid we'd get caught. Hadn't you noticed the bulge? Here. Rip it in shreds." The three women stirred the shredded paper into the coal paste, producing a thick, unreadable mash. Maman showed Eponine how to scoop up a handful and form it into a black ball the size of an egg. After it dried in the sun, they could use it in the stove as fuel.

"Clever, no?" Barbe Willocque said. "We use the paper twice. First we read it for information. Then we burn it, for heat. Both are acts of resistance against the Germans."

"Very clever," Eponine agreed. "But I wish I hadn't stolen the coal from the Salomons. They might need it themselves when they come back."

The house guest smiled. "Don't worry. You are helping the Salomons by making these balls."

"Whatever we do against the Germans helps the Salomons," Maman added quickly.

They listened to the radio together that night, and then Eponine went up to her room and pulled down her blackout curtain. She was glad to see the stars gleaming defiantly against the lingering dusk.

Eponine was almost asleep when she heard the soft sound of bare feet crossing her floor. She felt the bed sag as Barbe Willocque sat on the side of it.

"Are you still awake?" the house guest asked.

"Yes," Eponine said. "I was thinking. I'm glad you found something for me to do. I may be small like Maman, but like Maman I want to play my part."

"Good for you," Barbe said. "You obeyed, even when the orders didn't make sense to you. Tomorrow morning, before school, I shall give you your second assignment. It will be much more dangerous than the first."

These weren't words Eponine wanted to hear.

CHAPTER SEVEN
DAWN RIDE

Eponine lay awake all night, twitching with dread at what she might be asked to do. When Madame Willocque came in the next morning she was already dressed and sitting on the edge of her bed. Madame picked up the limp cloth horse from the floor and handed it to Eponine.

"I know it's childish, but it gives me comfort," Eponine said as she stuffed it beneath her pillow.

"We must all find comfort where we can. It's a rare commodity in this day and age." Madame stared out the window at the stars fading into the pale platinum of the eastern sky. She held a basket, which made Eponine wonder if she had worried for nothing. She wasn't afraid of delivering food to Father Simon. "I noticed last night that you had taken down your black-out blanket, but I was too preoccupied to ask why."

"You and Maman don't have one up."

"We must watch for certain things."

"Maybe I shall have to watch now, too."

Madame Willocque put a hand to her eyes as if rubbing the starlight from them. "You are taking on adult responsibilities with adult consequences. I must not treat you as a child. Call me Barbe." She held out her hand. Eponine shook it. Barbe's skin felt as dry as an autumn leaf, but her grip held strength and determination.

"Tell me what to do."

Barbe took a deep breath. "It's very simple, really. You mustn't be frightened or show fear."

"I'll be very brave," Eponine said, imagining the worst.

Barbe nodded. "I know you will. What you must do is ride Galopin through the fields to Reviers. Go all the way through town, then turn back and come home on the road. Take this basket."

Eponine peered inside at tiny, spring potatoes. Dirt still clung to their thin red skins. "Who do I give it to?"

"No one. On the way back to Amblie, you may pass a man walking on the road. Don't look at him. Don't acknowledge him. Get in front of him and allow him to follow you. At the stairs to Saint Pierre's, drop the basket. Pick up the potatoes, then come home."

"That's it?"

"That's it."

Eponine let out of a sigh of relief. "Who is this man?"

Barbe shrugged. "None of us knows any more than we need to."

"Dropping the potatoes makes no sense."

Barbe smiled. "As much sense as elephants on the moon."

Eponine smiled back. "Ah! A sign."

Barbe's smile broadened. "You know too much. Now get going or you'll miss your rendezvous."

Pleased to be out in the early dawn, Galopin pranced through the field as proudly as a show horse on parade. He had a smooth gait, even when he brought his feet up high. The chill morning air, heavy with dew, made Eponine feel alert. Off in the hedges a thousand birds twittered, arguing jocularly among themselves about who had been the early bird. I beat you all, Eponine thought.

They turned onto the gravel road. Galopin's hooves suddenly sounded very loud. The white bleached stones of Saint Vigor's church glowed. Eponine wondered if Father Bertrand was already up, preparing for matins. She was sure that, back in Amblie, her Father Simon wouldn't be at St. Pierre's yet. He wasn't an early riser, not as ambitious as Father Bertrand. Eponine giggled, remembering Father Simon rushing past on his way to early morning mass: late and disheveled, his hair uncombed. Maybe that was why he was a priest for the tiny village of Amblie instead of the town of Reviers.

The town slept. The windows on the houses' lower stories hid behind their shutters. The upper windows looked vacant and dark. A cat crossed the road on its way home from a night of prowling the alleys and streets in search of prey. It glared up at her a moment, its green eyes flashing like lamps, then disappeared behind a cluster of trashcans. Off in the distance, a rooster crowed.

Eponine came to the last house on the south side of Reviers at about the same time as the last star faded in the west. Sunrise was still a half hour away, but the sky brightened minute by minute. She rode up the hill and peered around. Fields stretched out in a broad, flat plain, but there was no single, walking man. Her heart thumping, she turned Galopin and cantered down the hill. Perhaps she was too late and had missed him. Galopin's hooves clattered through town, but no one seemed to notice. She passed the butcher's shop and the green grocer's. A dim light shone in the back of the Boivin sisters' shop. Eponine held her breath as she passed, hoping Marie and Marthe wouldn't look up from their dough and recognize her.

She passed out of town and followed the sunken road back toward Amblie. Her own village was close by when Galopin's ears pricked forward. A shadowy figure walked ahead, hidden in the depths under the trees. Had it not been for the horse, Eponine might have passed him without knowing. Bending down and stroking his neck, Eponine cooed comfort to Galopin. She glanced askance at the figure as she passed him at a trot and then slowed to a walk.

Except for the fact that he was unusually tall, he might have been any French farmer. The man wore a beret flat on his head. His shirt was old and torn at the elbows, his pants a little short for his long legs. He walked stiffly and awkwardly, as if he had covered a long distance in unfamiliar shoes. Eponine turned her head slightly so that she could see the man without looking at him directly. He was still following.

Eponine dropped the basket by the stairs to her little church. She slipped from Galopin's broad back and, muttering under her breath so that it looked convincing, picked up potatoes one by one and placed them back in the basket. She kept her back to the church and to the man, determined not to look at either, but out of the corner of her eye she saw the man hesitate briefly behind her, then bound up the stairs. The door to Saint Pierre's opened. Father Simon put an arm around the man's shoulders and guided him in.

Just as the sun sprang over the horizon, bathing the tree tops in golden light, the door closed. Eponine looked around, but to her relief there was no one with whom to share the glorious sight.

"Where's Barbe?" Eponine asked as she tossed the basket onto the kitchen table.

Maman didn't look up from the sink. "In the fields."

Eponine shook her head. "No she's not. Her straw hat's still in the cow shed." Maman raised an eyebrow at Eponine.

"I know," Eponine said with a laugh, "better not to know." She dunked the hard lump of bread into the bitter brew of ersatz coffee to soften it.

"Who was that man?" Eponine wondered aloud.

Maman's pursed lips hovered over her cup, blowing the steam away.

"A spy, maybe? Or a downed Allied pilot?"

Maman gave Eponine a searing look. "It's none of your business who the man was."

"But it is," Eponine said. "I took him to Father Simon."

Maman took a long sip from her cup before setting it down and running her fingers up and down her blouse as if making sure the buttons were all in place. "You didn't. You merely took your horse for an early morning ride."

"Is Papa working for the Résistance too? Is he hiding in the bushes, like the Maquisards?"

Eponine saw tears well in her mother's eyes, and went back to dunking her bread. "I'm sorry, Maman. I will ask no more. It's time for school anyway." She stuffed the heel of the bread into her mouth, gathered her books and escaped from her mother's misery.

The sun was high in the sky as she walked back through the fields. It felt good on her face, much warmer than it had an hour before, when she had ridden this way on her rendezvous with a stranger. She still didn't know who he was, but it didn't matter. She had done her part to aid the Résistance, and now everything looked different. The wheat in the field stood a little taller than yesterday, the sky was a brighter shade of blue. The air smelled sweeter. Eponine knew it was the smell of hope. Elated by what she had done, Eponine felt as if she were floating over the fields. She turned onto the gravel road and her spirits dropped back to earth. A German patrol marched along, going the same direction that she was. Eponine kept her eyes on the road and picked up her pace to avoid walking with them.

"It's my little horse rider!" one of the men said in perfect French.

Eponine looked up long enough to recognize the sergeant with the damaged face. The other soldiers grinned at her stupidly, making her quite sure that they hadn't understood their sergeant's words. Eponine flushed with pride and with power. What would he think if he knew she worked for the Résistance?

"And it's my knot-tying sergeant."

He smiled. The left side of his mouth curled while the right stayed taut. "I have a name. It's Johannes Hegel. And you are?"

Eponine opened her mouth to answer. A sudden thought stopped her. Didn't members of the Résistance have secret identities, like Ursule, to protect themselves? She wanted one, too. She searched her mind for a strong name, a name that had belonged to a woman who had also battled the enemy on her soil. "I'm called Jeanne," she said, taking the name of Jeanne d'Arc, the medieval heroine who had saved France from the English.

"Good to meet you, Jeanne. "You are, perhaps, twelve, no?"

Eponine smiled, neither denying nor accepting his guess. Let him think I'm twelve, she thought. It could be useful later.

"I guessed twelve because I have a granddaughter that age. You remind me of her. She loves horses, too. Perhaps after the war I could bring her here to visit. She would love this country."

Eponine's head snapped up. "You are in the army even though you are old enough to have a granddaughter?"

"I'm in the army again. I was in the Great War, too. Neither time by choice."

"My father fought in the Great War," Eponine said. "He was wounded. Burned, like you."

"I would like to meet him," the sergeant said. "We might have much in common."

Eponine sobered. "You can't. My father is building bridges somewhere."

"I'm sorry. You must miss him terribly." They walked without speaking. The crunch of gravel under the soldier's jackboots and the repetitive clink of a canteen against a belt buckle sounded like a dirge and a death knell.

The war had changed everything, even the school system in the French countryside. Amblie used to have its own school. Now the village children walked to Reviers. Classes had been consolidated, too. Where once there were separate classes, now boys and girls were jumbled into large, mixed-sex classes. Too many of the teachers had been conscripted into German construction crews or sent to work at ammunitions factories. Eponine didn't consider all the changes unwelcome. To conserve electricity and heating oil, students had every Thursday off. How the vacation saved fuel made no sense to Eponine, but she appreciated the holiday anyway.

Eponine slipped through the school gate without saying goodbye to her German escort.

"Will you look at that," Eponine's classmate, Sophie Junot said, "That foreign girl really does fraternize with the enemy. Just like Marie Boivin told my mother." Sophie's retinue of followers twittered like a flock of chickadees. Eponine looked into their hateful, burning eyes. She held her head high and walked past without trying to explain herself. The war hadn't changed everything. These girls had hated her before the Germans arrived in France.

She took her seat in Monsieur Le Doulcet's grammar class, but found it hard to pay attention. Eponine's mind wandered to her early morning ride. Surely the man was a downed pilot. She guessed that he was American. Yankees, she had heard, were taller than most Frenchmen. By the time Monsieur Thibault's math class began, the effects of a sleepless night were catching up with Eponine. Her head bobbed on her neck as she fought off sleep.

At ten o'clock the class filed into the dining hall for their snack of two vitamin- fortified cookies and skim milk. René elbowed his way through the milling students. He held out a chair and Eponine gratefully slipped into it. She gave the cookie a suspicious sniff.

"You know why they smell funny?" René asked. "They're made with fish meal imported from Latin America. Papa says they will keep us strong and ward away colds. Even so, I'm not sure I want to eat them."

Eponine choked it down. Her stomach hadn't always growled with emptiness. Then, perhaps, she would have preferred to go hungry and catch a cold than eat something that tasted so terrible, but that was long ago, before the Germans came. She ate René's untouched cookies, too.

Eponine's mind wandered through Monsieur Auber's Latin class. The school lunch: a small cup of skimmed milk, a scantily buttered slice of bread and a few teaspoons of meat and green vegetable did little to fortify her.

After lunch, Eponine made her way to her singing class. Behind her back the class called the teacher, Mademoiselle Pithou, "Fraulein Mouse" since she wore the same blue gray skirts and sweaters that German women who served in their military wore. Singing for Fraulein Mouse helped keep Eponine awake, but then it was on to Eponine's last class of the day: history and geography with the headmaster, Monsieur Couturier.

A big X of tape on the classroom window threw a cool, X-shaped shadow across Eponine's warm desk. The tape was supposed to keep the glass from shattering in a bombing raid. She wondered drowsily if her bedroom window should be taped since she wasn't going to hang the black blanket. Monsieur Couturier droned on, explaining how jackals in Africa cut a weak elephant from its herd before the kill. The shadow shifted, bathing her in warm light. Eponine's mind felt hazy and unfocused. Her thoughts flitted like the dust motes that danced in the sunlight, disappearing into shadow, then flashing out in a brilliance like shooting stars. She felt her mind fall into the darkness, then felt no more.

CHAPTER EIGHT
SOMEBODY'S WOMAN

For the second time that week Eponine woke to the sensation of someone shaking her. She sat up and found René hovering over her. Embarrassed, she wiped drool from her red-hot face.

"I must have dozed off," she murmured.

René nodded. "You are lucky you did so in Monsieur Couturier's class. He sympathizes with students' hunger sleepiness. Mademoiselle Pithou would have scolded you."

Eponine looked around the empty classroom. "Where is everyone?"

René chuckled. "You slept right through the bell. Come, let me walk you home. You don't look well."

Eponine reached for her books, but René grabbed them first. "I can carry these. You should eat an early supper and go to bed."

"Can't," Eponine said as they left the room. "I have to ride Galopin back to town to buy our food. Then there are chores to do, and homework."

"Let us get your food now and save you the trip."

Eponine stared at him dumbly. Her head felt like it was stuffed with wool. "I don't have my coupons."

René smiled. "I'm the mayor's son. Advantages come with status. Here. I will buy you a chocolate and a cookie. Enjoy them while I run your errands. The women of France must keep up their strength!"

He guided her into a cafe and settled her in, then disappeared out the door. Eponine nibbled on the cookie. The sign said it was a macaroon, but it tasted like sand and bran. The hot chocolate, a concoction of cocoa husks sweetened with saccharine, was hot and had the vague aroma of chocolate. Still, her mind cleared a little. Her thoughts grew less fuzzy. She was grateful that, despite his Pétainist exterior, René was still her friend.

"How did you manage?" Eponine asked when he returned twenty minutes later with three rations of bread and some meat.

René shrugged. "The shopkeepers gave them to me 'on credit' when I explained that you were ill. Monsieur Du Gouey felt so sorry for you that he threw in two extra sausages."

"Monsieur Du Gouey is too kind," Eponine said.

"Yes, he is," René answered. "He would get into trouble if the authorities knew he gave more meat than your allotment. But I won't turn him in. You need the food."

Eponine was shoving the food into her book bag when Sergeant Hegel walked in the cafe door. He clapped his heels together in a smart bow, pulling his field cap from his head. "Groceries so soon? You usually ride back for them later."

The hair on the back of Eponine's neck rose. Did he watch her routine that carefully? With a sudden panic, she realized that René might give away her true identity. How stupid she was to give a German a pseudonym.

"Mademoiselle doesn't feel well today," she said formally, hoping that would stop the conversation. "She is going home now."

The sergeant gave her a sympathetic look. "Would you like me to exercise your horse for you?"

"Thank you, but no." René placed himself between Eponine and the German. "We French can take care of ourselves."

And with that, he whisked her from the cafe.

René Bonté kept a firm grip on Eponine's elbow as he guided her out the door and up Reviers' main street. The rate that René was propelling her made it hard for her to walk normally. She had to take a little skip-hop every few steps to keep him from shoving her down. Eponine reviewed the situation in her mind. She wanted to slap herself for her naiveté. Sooner or later the sergeant would call her Jeanne in front of someone who knew her, or someone would call her Eponine in front of the sergeant. What kind of explanation could she come up with to avoid trouble when that happened? She would have to vary her routine and try to avoid Sergeant Hegel. She bit her lip until it hurt. They kept up this pace until they were out in the open fields, then René relaxed and dropped his hand.

"I don't like them paying attention to our women," he muttered. "That is our job."

"And you do it well," Eponine said breathlessly. "Thank you — for the groceries and the cookie and chocolate. You are very chivalrous."

René blushed scarlet. "But of course. It's the duty of the French man to uphold his woman."

Eponine laughed. "I'm not your woman, René."

"But you could be." His voice was so low that Eponine wasn't quite sure she had heard correctly. They walked along in silence, but Eponine's heart soared like the sparrows that flitted over the field. Her heart sang. For too long she had been the outsider, the one redhead in a village of brunettes, the Breton among Normans. Now the boy who had been among her few friends was offering her more than friendship – and he was the mayor's son at that! Eponine smiled, thinking of the looks on the other girl's faces when they realized that he had chosen her over them. She tilted her head back and let the warm sun play on her face to hide the red that had sprung into her cheeks.

When they arrived at Eponine's home René set her bag on the kitchen table and bowed first to one woman, then the other. He looked very formal and grave.

"Bonjour Madame Lambaol, Madame Willocque. I have delivered your daughter and your groceries. I must have ration coupons for the bread and meat. I promised the proprietors that I would return with them, and I'm a man of my word. I will attend to Galopin while you gather the coupons. Your daughter needs to rest."

He bent down and patted Madame Willocque's ancient white terrier on the head. "This is a sweet dog. What is his name?"

"Pétain." Barbe put a hand to her mouth to suppress a coughing laugh.

René looked up. "You must be very loyal to honor our grand old man by naming your dog after him."

Maman watched René pull the door shut behind him before she released her breath. "That young man likes you."

"Oh, Maman! You are being silly!" Eponine felt the color rise in her cheeks.

"No, you are silly. René may be more than just a Pétainist. He may be an *indic*. If he is an informant, he could turn you in to the Gestapo."

"Hush. He might hear you." Barbe beckoned with her hand and Maman and Eponine brought their heads together. "He isn't very smart, thinking I honored his *Maréchal* by naming this decrepit dog after him! But he can be useful. On Thursday when there is no school, Eponine should take a trip to the seashore for her health. And René is just the person to escort her."

Eponine stared at Barbe. "But the seashore's in the Forbidden Zone."

"Exactly. Now have a good time and remember to tell me all about the sights when you get back." Barbe winked. Eponine realized what she was being asked to do. She smiled. Tomorrow she was going to ask the mayor's son on a date.

CHAPTER NINE
HOLIDAY

E ponine sipped her ersatz coffee. "It's bright and clear."
　　"Perfect for a trip to the beach," Barbe added.

Maman frowned and ran a hand over her hair. "I will never forgive you for getting her into this. Who knows what kind of danger she might encounter in the Forbidden Zone." The Forbidden Zone ran inland several miles along the entire coast of Normandy. Within its well-guarded perimeters the Germans were building the largest collection of steel reinforced bunkers and gun emplacements that the world had ever known. Its secrets were well guarded.

"Relax," Barbe said. "Eponine is young and smart and pretty. You of all people should know that pretty can get you out of whatever smart can't."

Eponine smiled at her blushing mother. "I wish you could have seen René when I asked him. He strutted about the schoolyard like a pigeon, explaining how difficult it was going to be to get the proper passes. But he could do it. He was the mayor's son! He had connections!"

"Just don't expect me to be nice to him," Maman said. "I don't trust that boy."

As promised, René arrived at the doorstep when the bell of St. Pierre's tolled nine. Eponine studied his carefully combed hair and his Sunday-best tie and felt her face flush with pleasure. He held a bouquet of lilies of the valley. Eponine surmised from his damp trouser knees that he had plucked the flowers from the riverbank minutes before.

René offered the bouquet to Maman. "I take your flower for the day, and leave these in her place, though they aren't as sweet or as pretty."

Maman turned scarlet. Her hands fluttered about indecisively before accepting the flowers. Eponine gawked at her mother. A simple bouquet had won her over! How her opinion would flip back if she heard one of René's ridiculous speeches about how much good the Germans were doing for France.

René broke into Eponine's thoughts. "Papa tells me I must be polite to women. It's what our *Maréchal . . .*"

"Yes, well, no time for idle chit chat. Have a wonderful day. Be home before the sun sets." Barbe pushed Eponine and René out the door. René looked shocked at the abruptness, but Eponine smiled at him so sweetly that his confusion melted.

"Your father's cousin was very smart to propose this holiday," he said as he followed Eponine into Galopin's stall. "The seaside does wonders for one's health."

"She knows these things," Eponine said as she slipped the bit into Galopin's mouth. "After all, she was very sick. That is why she looks so boney, why her hair was cropped."

"That is what I had heard. Still, I wondered," René said. He awkwardly mounted Galopin, took the reins in his hands, then patted the horse's broad rump. "Well, then. Come on."

Eponine crossed her arms and frowned. "Why should you be in the front? He's my horse."

"But I'm the man. I should hold the bridle."

"They are reins, René. I question your horsemanship if you don't even know the terms." Eponine lifted one eyebrow and glared at René. After a moment he sighed, rested the reins on Galopin's neck and scooted back. René patted the place he had vacated. Eponine climbed up.

"Ugh! This is hard with you in the way!"

"I'm sorry," René said. "I only thought . . . well, never mind what I thought. I wish I could ride Hortense instead of doubling up on Galopin, but as long as we are together let's make a good day of it."

They rode down rue de l'Église and turned onto the road that headed north toward the coast. In the distance the sea looked like a gray ribbon against the blue sky. Eponine scanned the water. There used to be many boats out there: fishing boats and boats filled with cargo plying the waters between Oustreheim and Plymouth. The water was empty now. Mines and u-boats made them too dangerous.

They neared the first checkpoint and Eponine felt her heart thunder in her chest. She wished that she had allowed René to be in front so that she could hide behind his broad back. To get into the Forbidden Zone, one needed a bewildering array of stamps and signatures added to one's identity card, none of which she had. René flashed a letter signed by the *Préfecture de Police*. The guard waved them through without a word.

Eponine noted that the fields on either side of the road were waterlogged and René explained that the Germans flooded the fields to stop paratroopers from landing in them, to make the land more defensible. In another field a sign warned that the field had been mined. Eponine shuddered. Although it had never appeared in the papers or on the government-sanctioned radio news, rumor had it that a girl in nearby Lion-sur-Mer had stepped on one and had been blown into bits so small nothing remained to put in a coffin.

"Oh, look! Poppies" René slipped off Galopin's back, ducked under the fence and raced through the fields. Eponine tried to call him back but terror had turned her to stone. Her breath caught in her throat. She closed her eyes but she couldn't dispel the terrible image of bits of René flying through the air. She braced herself for the explosion which never came.

"Here."

Eponine opened her eyes and René offered her the fist full of blood-red flowers. She reached down a shaky hand. "You might have died,"

René chuckled. "Not in that field. My brother says that General Rommel commanded his men to lay 14,000 mines, but the troops had neither the mines nor the time to lay them before he was to inspect. Where they didn't lay mines, they posted signs."

"What if you were wrong? What if they had posted signs and laid mines both?"

René pointed to the black and white Norman cows that grazed contentedly in the field. "If there were mines in that field, those cows would be blown to bits. Wherever you see a cow, you may be sure that the pasture is safe."

Eponine tucked this tidbit of information away. She would report it later. "I still think you were very brave. I want to be brave, too. I want to help my country."

"But you are a girl," René scoffed. He grunted as he pulled himself up behind her, and then Eponine put her heels into Galopin's flanks and they continued on.

"Women have always helped defend France," Eponine said. "Take, for instance, Jeanne d'Arc."

"Women fight only when their men fail to be manly. As long as men do their job, then women can stay home and do theirs."

"You are impossible!" Eponine laughed.

They crossed a narrow stone bridge and entered the busy beach town of Courseulles. Thousands of men had dug the foundations and poured the concrete for the bunkers they passed. Although most were Russian and Polish prisoners of war, Eponine knew that some of those men were conscripted Frenchmen. They passed a half-finished gun emplacement swarming with workers and Eponine craned her neck searching for hair as red as her father's. She brushed aside the thought, shamed by the childishness of her hope. Surely if her father were so close she would have heard from him. He must be building bridges much farther away than Normandy's coast.

German cars and motorcycles whizzed past. Eponine tried to memorize the maze of narrow streets and stone buildings that radiated out from the Place de la Mairie. Just like Amblie, the houses of Courseulles were two and three story stone structures surrounded with little kitchen gardens and orchards. Apple blossoms were opening here. In Amblie they hadn't begun to open. One water tower and a church steeple stuck up through the trees. She noted the location of the town hall and the school. A train passed on the single track that ran parallel to the ocean. Painted on the engine was the slogan *"Rader Mussen Rollen Fur Den Sieg."* Eponine said the words aloud, trying to memorize them in case they meant something important.

"The wheels must turn for victory," René said. "You really should take German. It will be an important language to know in the New France."

Eponine shrugged. "I will take German in the fall if the war is still going on."

"You will need it even more if the war is over," René asserted. "Papa says it will be the language of international commerce, of letters, of science. It will be the most important language in the world."

"Next to French?" Eponine couldn't see him behind her, but she could almost feel the heat of his blush.

"But of course."

The train finally passed and they continued to the promenade, a broad concrete walkway set behind a low wall. The beach itself was flat and sandy. Eponine took note of the ten foot seawall. It would give an invading army trouble.

German officers filled the beach itself. Eponine watched them shout at the small flotilla of boats just offshore. A wave of men poured from the boats and waded ashore, shrieking wildly and throwing themselves on the sand. Once they were out of the surf they crawled on elbows and knees, their guns held before them.

"Papa says they are preparing for the invasion of England," René said.

The Germans didn't seem to mind their presence, so René and Eponine slid off Galopin's back and walked up and down the beach. Everywhere they went Germans drilled and practiced getting out of boats. Farther north, Eponine saw dunes behind the beach that bristled with enormous gun barrels. They passed a couple of cement gun emplacements, then decided to return to Courseulles for lunch.

The waitress eyed them suspiciously. "You have your ration books, no?"

"But of course," René said, producing his. Eponine got hers out, too. Food, even in restaurants, required coupons in addition to francs. They ordered one of the nicest meals Eponine had tasted in months. Here in the Forbidden Zone, where Germans outnumbered Frenchmen, food was of better quality and more plentiful. René chattered happily throughout the meal, but Eponine only caught snippets of it. She was too busy trying to memorize everything outside the restaurant window. The strain of trying to remember every detail weighed heavily on her. She felt as if her head was so stuffed with sights and sounds that she could see and hear no more.

"You look exhausted," René said. "Let us go back to the beach and sit in the sun for a while. Then I will take you home."

Eponine nodded. She had seen enough. They took their seats on the seawall and watched a company of German soldiers solemnly march to the beach, singing as they came. Eponine thought that Mademoiselle Pithou, her school's 'Fraulein Mouse' would have been teary-eyed with joy over their beauty and discipline. The soldiers stripped out of their uniforms, revealing very short, red swimming trunks and then dashed to the sea like children. None seemed able to swim. After a short while a sergeant blew a whistle and the men rushed back to land, where they sat in a circle and sang again.

"Can you understand?" René asked. "They are singing *Wir fahren gegen Engelland:* We are marching on to England."

"Enough," Eponine said. "It makes my head whirl." She wasn't lying. How was she ever going to describe everything that she had seen? They gave Galopin one last drink from the fountain in the town square, then crossed the bridge and left Courseulles behind. The land rose up in broad arcs between the rivers that flowed to the Atlantic, every tiny village marked by the heavenward thrust of its spire. The afternoon sun beat down on the road, making it shimmer in the distance. Eponine had to fight hard to keep her eyes open.

"It has been a good day," René said, somewhat drowsily. "I hope it has done you some good."

"Oh, it has," Eponine replied.

"I was thinking you and I should go out again. Papa says the movie theater in Caen is showing a very important film entitled *Le Juif Suss.* We should prepare ourselves for it by seeing the traveling exhibit on racial characteristics showing at the old labor exchange building."

"I don't think so, René. Thank you anyway."

"It's important you recognize the Jew," René said. "They are infiltrating our culture, taking our jobs. They want to ruin our economy by charging high prices for shoddy merchandise. They have no work ethic, no morals. We must rid France of them."

Eponine considered her words very carefully for quite a while before she spoke. "Wasn't Sarah Salomon's father your father's tailor?"

"But yes! He was," René said.

"A good man? Who traded fairly?"

"Always fairly."

"And were the suits well made, and at a fair price?"

"But of course," René said. "My father won't have patronized him otherwise."

Eponine pulled Galopin to a stop. She turned and looked René right in the eye. "You know, don't you, that the Salomons are Jewish?"

René looked as if he was going to fall off Galopin's rump. His mouth opened and closed several times before something came out. "Is that why Sarah isn't in school?"

"One may assume," Eponine said with a shrug. "As far as the Jews taking our jobs, I haven't seen anyone step forward to be the new village tailor. Your father must go all the way to Caen or Cruelly for clothes now, right?"

"When he can get them at all," René answered.

Eponine took one swallow before she moved in for the kill. "And whose fault is that, René? The Jews, or the Nazis?"

René didn't say another word all the way home. He was thinking, and that made Eponine happy. There was hope for him still.□

CHAPTER TEN
ERRORS IN JUDGMENT

The cone-shaped shadow of the village well stretched out long and blue when Eponine dropped René off at the Mairie and proceeded up rue de l'Eglise to her home. She brushed down Galopin and topped off his water bucket before entering the house. At the table sat her mother, her house guest, and a strange man. He was short and gray, much older than Maman and Barbe, with a tired face that matched his wrinkled suit. He stood and extended his hand.

"This is monsieur Moreau," Maman said. "He wants to hear what you saw today."

"Oh! A lot" Eponine dropped into a seat and tried to organize the flurry of sights and sounds that ricocheted through her mind. "The road to Bayeaux was packed with cars flying Nazi flags and transports filled with soldiers."

"Wehrmacht or SS?" Moreau asked.

"I don't remember, but there were a lot of them. And I saw a train running along the tracks that go along the coast between Courseulles and Bernières and it said 'the wheels must keep turning,' and there were lots of soldiers on the beach. They can't swim but they sing beautifully. They were singing about going to England, and they were singing the hunter's chorus from Weber's *Freischütz*. I know that song because my singing teacher, Mademoiselle Pithou, taught it to the boys. She says it's a manly song. Those soldiers made it sound good."

"How many soldiers were there?" he asked.

"Oh, a lot," Eponine said. "Too many to count."

"And gun emplacements. Did you count them? Can you tell me the calibers of the guns?"

Eponine blinked. "What's a caliber?"

Monsieur Moreau put his elbow on the table. He rubbed his eyes with his thumb and forefinger. "Madame, your daughter is a good escort for downed pilots. She sees nothing suspicious."

Maman's face reddened and Eponine knew that she had just been insulted. She felt like a child who hadn't done her chores correctly. Frustration and embarrassment forced tears into her eyes. She had seen so much. What had she missed that was important? Failure pressed down on her.

"It's my fault," Barbe said. "I didn't prepare her adequately."

"Give me another chance," Eponine said. "Give me a list of questions you want answered and I will look for the correct information. There was just so much to see!"

He picked his hat off the table. "I know, mademoiselle. It's not your fault. But I need to use all my people where they are the most help for the cause. Not everyone has a keen power of observation. Now, if you will excuse me, I must be back in Caen before nightfall."

"One moment, Monsieur!" Eponine searched her memory for something – anything — that would be of use. "Do you know the connection between mines and cows?"

Moreau was at the door when he turned. "The connection between mines and cows?"

"Rommel came to inspect before his troops put in the mines they were supposed to, so they put up signs to fool him into thinking they had done their job. If you see cows in the field, you may be sure that the pasture is safe, regardless of what the sign says."

Moreau raised his eyebrows. "Now that is interesting. And how did you learn that?"

"The mayor's son told me," Eponine said.

Monsieur Moreau winked at Eponine. She knew that she had done well.

Her next assignment came just a few days later. Again, she took Galopin out in the early morning hours, planning to drop a basket of potatoes then come home. This time, Eponine heard the man before she saw him. She was still in Reviers, walking Galopin through the dark streets when she heard whistling loud enough to be heard over the clop of Galopin's hooves on cobblestones. Eponine stopped. What she heard made her shudder.

The man wasn't whistling one of Jean Sablon's popular tunes, or Charles Trenet's, or a slow, sad song by Edith Piaf. He whistled a big band tune, the kind the BBC played. Please, Eponine thought, let him be a zazou – one of those crazy French boys who had adopted a strange style of dress and listened to American music in defiance of French ordinances.

She pressed Galopin into a trot. She could see the man now. He walked slowly and with a distinct limp, his hands rammed deep in his pockets. As Eponine passed him, she glared at him, pressing her fingers to her lips. He must have gotten the hint, for he stopped whistling. Eponine breathed a sigh of relief.

The moment that Eponine had glared at the man gave her a good view of his face. Like the last walker she had accompanied, he was tall and lanky. Brilliant, carrot red hair stuck out from under his beret and the dirt smudged on his face could not hide the freckles splashed across the bridge of his nose – freckles like hers. But it was his eyes that caught Eponine's attention. Like hers, and like her father's, they were hazel green.

She walked Galopin slowly, on occasion glancing back surreptitiously to make sure he followed. Every time she did, he smiled, his teeth gleaming in the darkness. Eponine shook her head. This one was incorrigible. After a while, he began jingling the coins in his pockets.

ching ching.

ching ching.

The sound jangled against Eponine's nerves like old Monsieur Auber's chalk against the board as he wrote Latin verb declensions. Frenchmen didn't jingle the change in their pockets.

They passed into the deep-set lane where the darkness of the trees swallowed up dawn's glimmer. Eponine couldn't hear the raucous call of the birds in the trees over the sound of the clinking coins. Exasperated, she drew Galopin to a halt and turned to face the man.

"*Non*," she said, mimicking the action of his hands in his pockets. "*C'est très amèricain.*" She mimed pulling her hands from her pockets. "*Bon*," she said.

He pulled his hands from his pockets. "*Mercy, bow coup, Madame-mua-zelle*," he said.

Eponine giggled. He had the worst pronunciation she had ever heard. Nevertheless, she was proud of the young man with the green eyes for even trying. She continued the slow ride to St. Pierre's church, where she dropped the basket just as planned. The man limped up the stairs, leaning on the stone balustrade. When he reached the top, he turned and waved at Eponine. "Arv-o-are," he said.

Eponine turned her head aside and giggled. The man didn't seem to notice that she was ignoring him. He was still waving when Father Simon came out of the church, grabbed him by the elbow, and forced him inside.

She was still giggling when she led Galopin into his stall.

"What's so funny?" A voice asked.

Eponine jumped so high she nearly slammed her head into the top of the horse stall. She whirled around and found René Bonté, the mayor's son, seated on the milking stool.

"What are you doing here?" she asked.

"Waiting for you."

"Why?"

He gave a sly smile that made Eponine even more nervous. The red which always seemed to linger on his cheeks darkened. Had René watched her guide the American to Father Simon? The mayor's house was just across the crossroads from the stairs to the church. If he'd looked out his window he would have gotten a good view of her and the American and still have had enough time to travel the short distance to her barn while she picked up potatoes.

René slipped from the stool. He leaned against the post and smiled his most debonair smile. He really was devastatingly handsome. "I came to walk you to school. These are dangerous times. A lady needs an honorable escort."

"I haven't eaten breakfast yet."

"That's what your mother said when I knocked on your door. I caught her in her bathrobe, poor thing. She looked much shaken. Say, I didn't know you rode your horse in the morning. How early do you get up?"

Eponine breathed a little easier. René wasn't smart enough to lie this smoothly. "I think better in school if I have done something physical beforehand."

"Good for you," René said. "Papa says the women of France must be physically strong if they are to participate in her rebuilding."

Eponine snorted. "That's me. Physically strong. Good things come in small packages, you know."

"Ah, but you have wide hips. Papa says that you would be good at carrying babies."

Eponine gave René a sharp look. She didn't like the idea that René and his father discussed her like some farm animal. She was not a brood mare. She smacked Galopin's curry brush into his hand. "You brush down Galopin while I eat breakfast."

Maman fluttered about the kitchen flapping like an old broody hen while Eponine assured her that everything was all right. By the end of breakfast the mayor's comments about her breeding ability seemed like another of René's silly jokes. It was still early when René and Eponine walked up the road to Reviers, so they took their time, strolling like the couples Eponine remembered seeing in the parks of Paris. René shifted all their books to one arm and put the other around Eponine's waist. Walking that close felt awkward, but delicious at the same time. Their hips bumped and collided until they found a way to match strides with each other, then it felt almost as if they were dancing, their bodies in sync. Eponine felt the gentle pressure of René's fingers against her waist, felt the warmth of his body radiating into hers. She looked up and he smiled, his dark eyes glowing like burnished chestnuts.

"Isn't spring beautiful?" René asked. "A good time for fresh starts." René's enthusiasm made Eponine smile. Dew glittered like strands of diamonds along the grass blades on the side of the road. The air smelled fresh, as if revived in the night. A cacophony of birds twittered in the trees. It really was beautiful.

"What fresh starts?" she asked.

"This is what I mean." René stopped walking and pulled her close to him. She felt his hand spread in the small of her back, supporting her. He leaned down and nuzzled her nose with his own in a gesture so tender that she felt her resistance melt. He kissed her, his lips soft and hesitant against hers. Eponine's knees grew weak as she leaned in to him.

"Pétain says the women of France must do penance for past indulgences," René whispered.

Eponine pulled her face away from his. "What?"

"The women of France have forgotten their place, which is in the arms of her young men. It's time to rebuild. France needs more babies." He pulled her closer and pressed his mouth to hers again, but this time Eponine didn't melt into his embrace. Rage welled up in her. She pushed against his chest.

"René Bonté, you pig!" she snapped. "Give me my books."

René blinked in confusion. "What have I done?"

"Being your girlfriend is one thing. Being your brood mare is quite a different matter!" Eponine ripped her books from René's arm, scattering his along the roadside. She ran all the way to school.

Barbe Willocque slammed the door when she came in for dinner that evening. Her face was livid, the skin pulled tight in anger. She opened her mouth to speak, but her coughing overtook her. Eponine watched the bony woman double up, hacking and coughing so violently that she was afraid the woman's lungs would turn inside out. Finally it stopped. Barbe dropped limply into a chair. "Father Simon tells me that you and the young man you led this morning developed quite a relationship."

"A relationship?!" Maman shrieked. "What do you mean?"

Eponine rolled her eyes. "I said a few words to him. I would hardly call that a relationship."

Barbe slammed her fist into the table. She brought her face, still red with coughing, so close to Eponine's that Eponine could smell the sour smell of her breath. "You aren't to talk to the men you lead. You aren't even to look at them."

"But he was acting stupidly," Eponine explained. "He would have given himself away with his whistling and his coin jingling."

Maman began sobbing – a slow, quiet sound like the leak of air from a tire that has gotten a pinprick.

Barbe ran a hand over her face. "If he wants to act stupidly and get caught, that is his business. But you aren't to jeopardize the operation by getting caught, too. You are to ride ahead of the men, without acknowledging them in any way. And if they are stopped by a patrol, you continue to ride. Never looking back, never noticing that anything unusual is happening behind you. You are just a young girl, coming home with a basket of potatoes you have just dug from the fields, fresh for breakfast. Do I make myself clear?"

Eponine cast her gaze to the ground. Heat rose in her cheeks. "Yes, Madame. I understand."

It was a long minute before anyone spoke. Maman's sobs pierced Eponine's heart.

"Good," Barbe said. "If I can't trust you, I won't give you any more assignments. You could get all of us killed." She crashed her weight into a chair, letting her legs sprawl out in front of her. "I also hear that you spurned the mayor's son this morning."

Eponine felt her face flush. "Who did you hear that from?"

"It's all over the village," Maman said tearily. "The other mothers think you are a fool. That smug Madame Junot thinks that now her daughter Sophie has a chance to catch the mayor's son."

"Well, let her," Eponine snapped. "René is the fool. I want nothing more to do with him."

Barbe grabbed Eponine by the blouse and dragged her close. "René's brother Jacques is high in the French Militia and desperately wants to earn the admiration and favor of the SS and the Gestapo. Anger the Bontés and you will have them all breathing down our necks."

Eponine finished her meal in silence, then crept to her room. She lay on her bed, feeling battered and bruised by Barbe's words. Overhead in the attic the mice scuttled to and fro, but she dismissed the sound. She had a lot to think about, all of it very, very serious.

If only her father would return, she thought. He would save them.□

CHAPTER ELEVEN
ANSWERS

The next morning Eponine swallowed her pride and sought out René in the school yard. She felt the eyes of her classmates boring into the back of her head and turned to meet their gaze. Some looked at her with disgust, as if looking at a slug or some other primitive form of life. Others looked curious, not knowing what to make of her red hair and freckles. But no one looked friendly. Eponine felt like a freak at the circus.

Sophie Junot scowled out from her crowd of friends as Eponine walked by. "I wouldn't bother René if I were you, not that I would ever be you. I would rather die first." The gaggle of girls giggled.

Eponine's hands curled into white knuckled fists. She turned and faced Sophie. "I'm not going to bother him. I'm going to apologize."

"You had your chance with him," Sophie said in a growl. "Let someone else – a real French girl – befriend him now. We French women know how to please our men."

"I'm French," Eponine said through her teeth.

Sophie turned towards her cohort of followers. "She doesn't even know who or what she is," she said, then turned on her heel and the group moved off. Eponine stared after them. Sophie was more right than Eponine wanted to admit. She wasn't sure who or what she was. She wasn't sure if she wanted to ask for René's forgiveness. But she had to. Barbe Willocque demanded it.

She moved towards René, who stood at the far side of the school yard. His turned his back to her, ramming his hands deep into his pockets and hunching his shoulders into an impenetrable wall of angry resistance. But Eponine was determined to find a chink in his armor and breach it.

"René," she said softly, "I came to apologize."

René gave a taciturn grunt. He stared sullenly at his shoes, offering neither encouragement nor rejection.

"I'm not used to men's advances," she said when the silence had stretched itself out awkwardly. "I miss the friend you used to be – the friend who rode with me and joked with me."

"He doesn't exist anymore," René said. "He grew up."

"Too quickly for me."

"There's a war going on, or hadn't you noticed? Wars make boys grow up fast." His dark brown eyes filled with confusion. "Fast, and desperate. If I don't grow up, I might miss the whole thing. You didn't know that about me, did you? You thought I was just a rich, silly boy, happy to remain idle throughout the war. But I'm not. How can you miss me when you don't even know me?" He turned and walked away. Eponine watched his hunched shoulders retreat, but she didn't dare go after him.

Days passed.

Eponine's life fell back into its usual routine. She woke early and did her chores, then walked to school alone. René didn't visit the stable again, but over time he relented, first with glances in her direction, then with tentative smiles. Eponine smiled back. She missed his companionship. She felt even more alone and isolated from her classmates now that she had lost both Sarah Salomon and René Bonté.

Eponine became conscious of the subtle undercurrents that ran through her teacher's lectures. Fraulein Mouse, the singing teacher was a collaborationist, working to instill Germanic values in her students. The headmaster, Monsieur Couturier, was clearly sympathetic to the Résistance, as was her Grammar teacher, Monsieur Le Doulcet. She wasn't sure about Monsieur Thibault, the math teacher, but could tell that the Latin teacher, Monsieur Auber, approved of neither Pétain's government nor De Gaulle's Résistance fighters. No one but the Imperial Romans themselves would please him.

In the afternoons Eponine rode Galopin back to Reviers to pick up whatever foodstuffs she was allowed to buy. She watched for little cards in merchant windows announcing that today meat was allowed to Category A, which encompassed most adults including Maman and Barbe, or that Category J3, those aged 13 through 21, deserved extra bread from the Boivin Sisters, or milk from the crèmerie. Of course, just because she deserved them didn't always mean Eponine got them. One could only buy what the stores had to offer. If the shelves were empty, so was her stomach.

Sometimes she ran into the SS patrol. Usually she avoided them.

The Boivin Sisters continued to question Eponine's parentage, her morals, and her very purpose in being. Red hair, Marie and Marthe thought, was indicative of the devil's doings, which those pagans in Brittany were bound to be tied up in. Eponine just smiled. She had managed a few shady deals, not for the devil but for the Résistance, and she was proud of them.

She, Barbe and Maman slid into the coal cellar every evening to listen to encouraging news from Radio Free London. Although the Germans had recently posted flyers all over town depicting the Americans as a snail crawling slowly up the boot of Italy, the radio reported that American troops were nearing Rome at a rapid rate. The eastern front had collapsed in on itself, the Germans retreating out of Russia in ragged bands. Africa was firmly in the hands of the Allies.

Most of the time Eponine knew that the strange announcements: "Gentlemen, place your bets," or "The camel is hairy," were for other people in Paris or Rouen or on the border with Brussels. But sometimes Maman and Barbe gave each other a knowing look and Eponine knew that one or the other would slip out after curfew. She wasn't sure what they were doing, or where, but she had learned to accept this. It was better not to know.

After the radio broadcast, Eponine climbed the dark stairs to her bedroom, undressed in the darkness and slid between cold sheets. They felt good. May of 1944 was turning out to be one of the hottest on record, with little rain to beat down the dust. Overhead the mice scuttled through the attic while outside her window stars twinkled faintly in a sky where blue lingered a little longer each day. By June, the sky would stay lit well after ten o'clock.

Sometimes, late at night, she awakened to the drone of slow-moving bombers. When that happened she searched through her bedding for her old stuffed pony and held it tight, breathing in its stale, saw-dusty comfort. There seemed to be more bombers with each passing day. Usually they sounded far off, in the distance. Once, a sound like thunder had followed. Eponine learned the next day that the fortifications along the beach had been hit. Other nights, the planes passed directly overhead, their engines growling so deeply that she felt their vibrations in her chest. She scrambled to the window and looked for them but they passed like shadows against the dark sky, making the stars wink out as they went over. Other times the searchlights found them and the sky lit up in a spectacle of tracers and anti-aircraft fire that was a terrible delight to witness.

No one in Amblie worried much. They believed the bombers were searching for military targets along the coast and for the airfield near Caen, not their small village.

Insecurity crept into those twilight hours. She was only one very small girl in a very small town. Perhaps no more would be asked of her. Or had she performed so badly that the Résistance no longer trusted her? She waited for Maman to give her another assignment, but days slipped past. Eponine couldn't tell whether she was relieved or disappointed.

The bombing raids increased. She heard in school that American bombers flew by day, the British by night. Once, her Latin class left their seats and pressed to the windows to watch a bomber with its right wing sheared off plunge out of the sky. Five little white puffs followed in its wake, parachutes carrying men who had managed to bail out. Eponine hoped that she would cross paths with one of the five; guide him to a safe haven. It didn't happen.

She wondered what had happened to the two men she had guided. Out in the school yard students gossiped that some downed airmen took the long and arduous trek over the Pyrenees Mountains into Spain, where they still had to avoid Franco's troops before they found safe haven in Gibraltar. Others slipped over the border into Switzerland. Still others went to Brittany, where Breton fishermen took them out to sea and handed them over to the British. Eponine hoped that her men had gone that route. She somehow found comfort in thinking that she was part of a Breton underground. She knew nothing of the Breton language, had never been on Breton soil, but still they were her people.

Eponine thought about Sarah Salomon and her family. Where were they? Had they, too, been smuggled over a border, or had the Gestapo picked them up? The talk about round-ups grew more terrible every day. Someone told her that the Germans put a thick coat of lime on the floor of the trucks they used to transport Jews. As the lime got wet during the trip, toxic fumes rose up so that many died before they reached their destination. She passed this story on to René and found pleasure in how his face wrinkled in confusion. If these rumors were true, the Germans weren't the orderly peacemakers that he thought.

Like isolated pieces of a jigsaw puzzle, a few scattered memories of her father came back to her. She remembered him whistling American tunes while she rode his shoulders and he handed out fliers on the streets of Paris. She didn't remember what those fliers contained and she guessed that was because she hadn't yet learned to read. Had they been advertisements? Political tracts? She remembered digging her fingers into curly hair that glistened in the sun like spun copper. His green eyes sparkled out of his battered, mask-like face when he laughed. In her memory he was always laughing. Because of that, or perhaps because he was her father, she didn't remember being frightened of his scars.

She had always believed that he was very tall, like the men she had accompanied to St. Pierre's church, but was that because he actually was tall, or because she was so small when last she saw him?

Red hair. Green eyes. Tall frame. Karadeg Lambaol had looked more like the last man she had escorted than he looked like a typical Frenchman.

He didn't look like most of the Bretons she had met, either, although Eponine had to admit that she had met precious few Bretons.

Why was he gone so long building bridges?

Her questions about her father flowed like an underground river, running invisible to the outside world yet stirring up currents which eddied in her mind throughout the day. She found it hard to pay attention in class. She dawdled through her chores. At night, thoughts woke her from her dreams. She began to think that she couldn't rest or work effectively until she knew the answers, and that everything in her life would be well if she only she knew where – and who – he was.

Finally, one morning when the three women were at breakfast, Eponine's curiosity overflowed its banks. She set her bread down and studied her mother's face. "Maman, you must tell me about Papa."

Jacqueline Lambaol's head snapped back as if she had been slapped. Her cheeks flushed, but she said nothing.

"The Papa I remember looked more like the Americans I've taken to Father Simon than like anyone in Brittany."

Maman rearranged her silverware. "You've never been to Brittany. And what makes you think the men you've seen are Americans? They could be Canadians or Englishmen or Russians. They could be defecting Germans for all you know."

"You're avoiding answering my question," Eponine said.

"Answer her," Barbe said. "I think it's time."

Maman glared at Barbe. "You always think it's time. You're always pushing me, pushing her." She sighed. "Ah, very well. Your father was American. He fought for France during the Great War, before the Americans entered. That's when he burned his face."

Eponine edged to the front of her chair. Her heart pounded in her temples. It was as if the puzzle pieces of her memory were coming together and forming a picture she had only dimly perceived before. "Were you a nurse? Did you nurse him back to health? Is that why he stayed?"

Jacqueline Lambaol smiled as she shook her head. "Your father fell in love with France long before he fell in love with me. I was a student at the University when I met your father. He was handing out pamphlets on a street corner."

Recognition flashed through Eponine's mind. "I remember that."

"You weren't born yet, silly. You remember another time. Your father frequently handed out pamphlets."

"What kind of pamphlets? Was he a communist?" Eponine scrambled to sort out her memories, to make sense of them. She had more than scattered, isolated memories now, but her images remained confused. It was as if she had collected all the pieces within the box but they were still a jumbled, meaningless pile.

Barbe coughed and laughed simultaneously. "Why ask when you make up your own wonderful stories? A communist marries the nurse who helped him heal! You should be a novelist."

Jacqueline gave Barbe a wry look. "She should! Her story is better than mine. But no, Eponine, they weren't about politics. They were about God. Your father was a Protestant, and when I met him he was handing out fliers for what the Americans call a tent revival, in Luxembourg Gardens."

Eponine scratched her head. This didn't fit into her preconceived pattern at all. "I assumed we were atheist."

"My father was a minister in the French Calvinist Church – a minority if there ever was one. I was intrigued to meet a Protestant from another part of the world. I left all that behind when I moved you here. I thought it was safer."

"A mistake," Barbe interjected. "It is hard to live without the courage of your convictions and the comfort of your God."

Maman leaned forward. She looked intently into Eponine' eyes. "You really don't remember going to meetings? It was a small building with white walls. No gruesome, crucified Christ like at St. Pierre's. No priests in fancy garments. Just a simple cross, simple pews, simple songs."

Eponine shook her head. Her memories of church, if she ever had any, were gone. The puzzle of her memories still had missing pieces.

"You should teach her," Barbe said.

"When the war is over. There will be plenty of time then to learn about Christ and Calvinism," Maman said, but Eponine's thoughts had left the church behind.

"Was my father's father from Brittany?"

"You're not Breton. Your father's father, or his father's father, or something like that, was from Ireland. Your father had an Irish last name. But France was in an uproar. The communists were winning seats in the government. Opposing parties were instigating riots. The Germans were moving into the demilitarized zone. Resentment over foreigners in France, even Americans, was spreading. I gave us new names to protect us. I thought a Breton name would help explain your auburn hair and your green eyes."

Anger welled up in Eponine's chest. The countless times she had weathered the Boivin sisters' insults and defended Brittany had been pointless. Brittany meant nothing to her. Her puzzle lacked more pieces, and she had pieces which didn't belong to the puzzle at all. Eponine discarded the notion that she was Breton. A thought caught in her throat, sudden and stunning in its ramifications. "Am I Jewish? Is that why you and I are in hiding? Or Gypsy?"

"You are half Irish-American, half French. Neither Jew nor Gypsy."

Another panicky thought. Eponine felt the puzzle going to pieces again.

"Does father know our new names? How can he find us if we have aliases?"

A sad smile crossed Maman's face. "He knows them. He knows where we are."

"What is my real name?" Eponine asked.

Her mother was just about to answer when Barbe Willocque cut in. "You are a member of the Résistance. You have an alias."

Eponine almost said that she had an alias, that a German thought her name was Jeanne. She bit her lip and kept mum. It had been stupid to give Johannes Hegel a false name and she knew it. If Barbe and Maman found out, her role in the Résistance would be over. But it was intriguing to learn that Jeanne was not her only alias. Eponine was an alias. Her identity was buried deep within layers of secrecy and fear.

"After the war you can learn your real name and meet your relatives – and learn about God," Barbe added.

Tears of confusion and frustration splashed down Eponine's face. "But I want to know now. The more answers you give me, the more confused I am. I don't even know who I am anymore, why I'm in hiding. I don't know who my father is, or where he is, or what he's doing. How can I live with all these questions?"

Neither Maman nor Barbe reached a hand to comfort her. Neither offered her a reassuring word. She cried for a long time. The tears flowed unimpeded until they had soaked the front of her blouse and dampened the scrap of bread she held in her hand. Finally, when there were no more tears, Eponine hiccupped.

"If he knows how to find us, why doesn't my father, whatever his name is, come back?"

"Because he can't, or he would." Maman got up. Eponine watched the door close behind her mother before she turned her eyes to Barbe Willocque.

"Why can't he?" she asked. Something deep inside her dreaded the answer she feared she would receive.

Barbe shrugged her shoulders. "I know nothing about your father. I only met your mother when I arrived on her doorstep last winter. Go wash your face and go to school so I can join your mother in the fields. You have heard enough for one morning."

Eponine did as she was told, but she didn't believe she'd heard anywhere near enough. There was more to this story, and she was determined to learn it.

CHAPTER TWELVE
DISTINGUISHING FRIEND FROM FOE

When Eponine went for her bread that afternoon the soldiers were standing outside the Boivin sisters' bakery. Their faces were browner than they had been a few weeks ago. Obviously they enjoyed the long, warm spring days. Resentment bubbled in Eponine's stomach. She swallowed the urge to tell them to go back to their land of cold, harsh winters and sickly sweet white wines. They didn't belong here. Their presence ruined everything, even the weather. When had winters been as cold? When such hot, dry springs? The Germans were an aberration of nature.

"*Guten Tag*," the taller of the two soldiers said as she slipped off Galopin's broad back and led him the few steps to the railing. He frightened her more because he seemed most interested in her. The other busied himself with Galopin, cooing in the horse's ear and stroking his broad nose.

The tall soldier said something in German. Eponine shrugged her shoulders to show that she didn't understand.

She took a step.

The soldier stepped in front of her.

Eponine took a step sideways, to the left.

He matched her step.

She stepped right.

It was like an awkward country dance, where the couple mirrors each other's movements but never touch, but with each step, the German drew closer. Eponine felt the heat off his black wool jacket. The glare of his buttons and badges pierced her eyes. She put up a hand to block the light and the soldier grabbed her wrist. His grip was strong. Eponine grimaced.

"Nein," she said.

"Nein," the soldier echoed mockingly. He said something to his comrade, who laughed.

"Nein," Eponine repeated, unsure of what else to say. Before the soldier could respond, she heard another German voice, a voice she recognized. She couldn't understand what he said, but it was harsh and angry.

"*Scheisse*." The soldier dropped Eponine's arm and walked away. His buddy followed. Eponine threw herself into the arms of Johannes Hegel, the sergeant with the damaged face. Great sobs welled up in her throat.

"You saved me again."

"Don't cry, Jeanne." He wiped her cheeks with the back of his hand.

She looked up and saw him smiling out of the undamaged side of his face. The other side remained stiff, immobile. He looked like one of those drama masks that are half tragic, half comedic and suddenly she remembered that while he might be her friend and rescuer, he was also a German. Eponine pushed herself out of his embrace and folded her arms over her chest.

"What does that mean? The word he just said."

"*Scheisse?*" Sergeant Hegel's face clenched in distaste. "It means shit, if you will pardon my language. It means that he is very unhappy to be deprived of his chance to speak with a pretty girl. But he will get over it."

He glared after the retreating figures for a while, and then turned his smile back to Eponine. "The SS isn't regular army. They lack discipline. Our directives say we must treat all women, young and pretty or old and bent, with respect. I especially don't like that he is attracted to one as young as you. I will tell their superior to remind them."

Sergeant Hegel sighed and shook his head. "They wouldn't act like this if they were home with their own wives and mothers and sweethearts. I'm tired of this war. Tired of all wars."

The gravity in his tone made Eponine squirm. She felt awkward letting a German share his soul with her. To lighten the mood sarcasm sprang to her lips. "But you need to be here. You must protect us from the Red menace from the east and the capitalist menace from the west." Eponine winced. She sounded too much like René.

Sergeant Hegel grinned at her and jerked his chin toward the now-gone SS men. "Maybe they are here to do that. I'm here because I was drafted. I have no desire to be here. You see this?" He pointed at his belt buckle and his face grew serious again. "It says '*Gott mit uns.*' That means 'God is with us.' I wonder what kind of a God would side with us."

"Why is that?" Eponine asked.

Sergeant Hegel answered with a deep shudder. "Read *Mein Kampf* if you want to know." He sighed. "I want nothing more than to be done with all this."

Eponine stared at him. The damage to his face made his expressions difficult to read, but she thought he was sincere. "Why don't you just run away? Quit the army. Go into hiding until the war is over?"

He shook his head and laughed bitterly. "I would be shot, either by one side or the other. One can't run away unless one has planned in advance where one is to go. One must have friends."

The battered sergeant glanced at the sky. Longing crossed his face. "I hope I find that friend soon. The English and the Americans will be here within the month."

"Do you think so?" Eponine's her heart leaped. "Oh, I hope you are right."

He looked at her, his gray eyes pools of sadness. "It will be ugly when they come, many killed on both sides, civilian deaths as well. I pray, Jeanne, that you aren't among them."

She hardly saw the world pass her by as she rode home. Eponine mulled over the impending doom of Johannes Hegel as the Allies drew near. If he was guessing right about how the war was going, he would soon be in a terrible situation while Eponine and the other villagers would soon be liberated. And yet, Johannes Hegel was worried about Eponine. The selflessness of his concern melted her heart.

The fate of the German sergeant became entwined in her mind with her father's fate. If she could save the one, the other would be saved, too. Return Johannes Hegel safely to his family and Karadoc Lambaol would return to his. Eponine closed her eyes and took in a long, deep breath before she made a pledge to that God she was beginning to believe in. She would do all she could for the sergeant.

Eponine didn't say a word about her German soldier when she arrived home. There were already too many unanswered questions and points of friction between her mother, Barbe and herself. They ate uneasily, the clicking of fork against crockery as startling as gunfire in the sullen silence. The question of where her father was and why he didn't come home hovered over the table like smoke from a wet fire. Its bitterness made Eponine's eyes water, her throat tighten. What was her real name? It was pointless to ask. Maman had kept it secret a long time. Eponine couldn't remember being called anything but Eponine, couldn't remember being anyone other than a Breton. She searched her mind for a memory of who she had been before she left Paris, but it wasn't there. She remembered how the furniture was arranged in the apartment, the view out the window, the walk to the green grocer's and the bread shop, even the long stroll to the park. But she didn't appear in any of her memories, and no one leaned down and spoke her name to her.

Eponine finished her meager meal of rutabagas and carrots and stood to take her dishes to the sink when Maman stopped her.

"I'll do the dishes tonight. You take this to Father Simon." Maman handed Eponine a food package.

Eponine's knees went weak with relief. "You've forgiven me for talking to that American?"

"Your mother wants you to take a basket to Father Simon," Barbe interjected. "You don't need to know any more than that. Now go, before she changes her mind."

Eponine raced out the door, grateful that Maman and Barbe trusted her enough to transport supplies. She ran to the end of the street and then bounded up St. Pierre's uneven granite stairs two at a time. The door of St. Pierre's was locked. No lights shone in the windows. She ran to the rectory, where she found the housekeeper Madame Tournebulle snoring loudly in her chair by the stove, but no priest. Eponine raced back home.

"He isn't at either the church or the rectory," she said breathlessly.

The two women looked at each other before Barbe answered. "He might be at Saint Vigors."

"Visiting Father Bertrand?"

Maman's hands fluttered like wounded doves. "The Gestapo picked up Father Bertrand this morning, on suspicion of harboring fugitives. Father Simon now shepherds both the Amblie and Reviers parishes. But the basket must go tonight. Here. Let me take it."

Maman reached for the basket, but Eponine pulled it back. "Galopin would welcome the ride to Reviers."

Maman looked at Barbe, who shrugged. "Then go."

Eponine was out the door before either woman could change her mind.

Galopin trotted with his hooves held high, pleased to be out for a second time in an evening. Eponine didn't share his enthusiasm. Father Bertrand's arrest was too close. If she weren't careful, she could be next. Or Father Simon. Or Maman. Or Barbe Willocque.

She vowed to be even more careful around René Bonté and Johannes Hegel. Eponine twitched with nerves. The setting sun stretched out the shadows of the trees like dark corpses along the road. A member of the Gestapo might lurk around every corner. Eponine's heart made a sound like a stick beating dry sand in her ears. Saint Vigors, the parish church in Reviers, hid in the shadows of its own trees, its flat, white front tinged as pink as flayed flesh in the sunset. Eponine walked Galopin carefully through the clutter of fallen grave markers that littered the church grounds. The big doors in the front of the church were closed tight. No light gleamed in the windows. She rode around back. A thin line of yellow light seeped under the sacristy door. She knocked.

"Who's there?" Father Simon's voice sounded tremulous.

"Eponine Lambaol. With a care package for my cousins in Paris."

Eponine heard a chair drag across the stone floor, then the soft fall of footsteps. The door opened and Father Simon's face appeared, backlit so that it looked haloed in yellow light. Father Simon grasped Eponine by the elbow and quickly pulled her in before shutting the door behind her.

The sacristy was a tiny room, barely bigger than a closet. Eponine noticed a clothes pole draped with cassocks and robes. Stoles, one for each color in the church year, hung on a hook by the door. A crosier and a crucifix on a long pole leaned next to them. Eponine's gaze fell on a small desk piled with papers. Other papers lay strewn about the floor; as if someone had thrown them hither and yon while searching for something. She guessed that the Gestapo had made the mess and Father Simon had been restoring order when she knocked. He picked a handful of papers off the floor and set them on the desk.

"They took the radio. I don't know what else they got. It may take me quite a while to sort through this mess. I hope Father Bertrand didn't have any baptisms or weddings coming up that I don't know about."

Eponine handed him the basket. "I didn't cause Father Bertrand's arrest by talking to that American, did I?"

Father Simon lifted his eyebrows. "You knew he was American?"

"He was making it terribly obvious. I told him to pull his hands from his pockets and to stop whistling. I won't talk to another."

"Good," Father Simon said. "I won't want one of my parishioners endangering herself."

"I'm not your parishioner, you know. My mother and I aren't Catholic."

Father Simon shrugged. "You are my parishioners whether or not you are Catholic. Like Jeanne d'Arc, you listen with your heart to the voice of God. You do what is right. Before he was killed in the Great War, the poet Charles Peguy said 'In wartime, he who refuses to surrender is my friend, whoever he may be, wherever he may come from and whatever party he may belong to.' That applies to you and your mother."

The quote emboldened Eponine. "Might it apply to others as well?"

"But of course."

"Even a German soldier who is tired of war and wants to defect?"

Father Simon studied Eponine's face closely. "How would we know he wasn't a spy?"

"But what if he wasn't?"

Father Simon sucked in his lower lip and chewed on it thoughtfully. "This German isn't just a 'what if', is he? He is real?"

Eponine nodded. "He wants to defect."

Father Simon's face darkened. "So he tells you. But consider the timing here – asking to defect the day Father Bertrand was arrested. The Gestapo realized they made a mistake. Bertrand won't betray his comrades. They need another way to uncover our organization. That other way may be your German."

Eponine felt her jaw drop. "He is sincere."

"That is what it takes to be a good spy – the ability to act sincere."

"But that small voice that speaks to my heart, the one you said was like Jeanne d'Arc's voice, it tells me that this man is good."

"Fundamentally all men are good," Father Simon said, "but because of original sin they are also corrupt. And they can corrupt that still, small voice. I'm sorry. I cannot, will not, do anything for your German."

Eponine didn't say anything, but in her heart she knew that Father Simon was wrong. She would have to find another way to save Johannes Hegel.

CHAPTER THIRTEEN
THE SPY

The next morning Barbe shook Eponine awake. She handed Eponine a basket of potatoes. Eponine sat up and groggily stared at the platinum sky. After a night of tossing and turning, her dreams filled with leering SS men and the whine of Citroen engines, her head felt like it was stuffed with straw. Dread bubbled in her stomach. She fought it down, afraid that if she refused to go now she might never be given another chance. She reminded herself that she wasn't doing anything she hadn't done before. Eponine crawled out of bed. She dressed and went out the door before the eastern sky held a hint of pink.

She found the man walking in the deep shadows under the poplars where the road dipped into the little valley which hid the village of Amblie. It wasn't far from where she had encountered the maquisard who demanded her bread, and only meters from the stairs to St. Pierre's. Eponine sighed as she passed him. She wouldn't have to guide him very far at all, and then she would be home again, safe and sound, sipping ersatz coffee.

The air flowed down the hill, casting a breeze on her back. Heavy with dew under the overhanging branches, it felt chilly on her skin. She shivered. The warm, green smell of fresh horse droppings wafted up and Eponine knew that Galopin had just raised his tail and done his morning duty. Everything was as it should be.

"*Scheisse*," the man muttered.

Eponine pulled Galopin to a halt. She twisted around and saw him standing on one leg, peering at the bottom of his boot. Evidently the darkness under the trees had obscured Galopin's movements. He had stepped in the fresh pile.

But what had he said? Eponine knew that word. Johannes Hegel had taught her its meaning.

He looked up at her, his face red, and said something. It was unintelligible, but Eponine recognized its cadence as English, not German.

Eponine swallowed the hard lump in her throat. She had promised Father Simon that she wouldn't talk to this man. She had promised Barbe Willocque. But if she performed her task as usual and he was a spy, he would jeopardize the lives of everyone she loved. Her trembling hands on the reins were making Galopin skittish.

"I'm sorry, sir. I don't understand English," she said in French, hoping that he couldn't detect how her voice shook with terror. She couldn't let him know that she suspected him. If she were lucky, he hadn't even realized his own mistake. Even though her heart beat wildly, Eponine smiled before she turned back around. She prodded Galopin on, but slowly. She needed time to think. Her head didn't feel like it was filled with straw anymore. Ideas whirled through her mind so quickly that she couldn't grasp any of them.

A crow called in the woods. She and Galopin both startled. Then she realized that it was just the diversion she needed.

"Shhh." Eponine whirled around and placed her forefinger in front of her lips. "I hear something. Danger." She put her hand to her ear, miming her words. The man stopped, warily looking around. He looked as spooked as Galopin. She hoped it was because she had convinced him that danger lurked nearby. "You," she said, pointing at the man. "There," she said, pointing toward the bocage.

"*Moi?*" he asked, pointing a finger at his own chest.

"*Oui. Pendant un moment, seulement.*" Eponine wasn't sure if he understood exactly, but he crawled into the bushes.

Now if she could only keep him there until she got help. She tucked her heels into Galopin's sides and he bolted, but she hadn't gone more than a few feet before the man scrambled, shouting, from the bocage. He ran to her. She didn't understand his words, but she could guess that he was begging her not to leave him.

Eponine slipped off Galopin's back, setting her basket of potatoes carefully down. She pointed to the bush. "Danger," she said slowly and precisely, hoping he would grasp at least the basics. "You, go there. One moment, only. I leave horse. I go up the road." She used two of her fingers to pantomime walking. "I look for Germans, for danger." She placed her hand flat over her brow and turned her head back and forth, as if scanning the horizon. "I come back." Her fingers walked again. She tied Galopin's halter on a branch and then pointed once more to the bocage. He seemed to understand, and casting back a reluctant look, crawled into the shadows.

Her heart pounding wildly, Eponine ran down the rest of the hill. She scrambled up the disheveled church stairs as quickly as she could. At the top, she knocked on the door to St. Pierre's with a shaking fist. The door opened and Father Simon stared out at her, a look of bewilderment on his face.

"Eponine? What . . . ?"

"No time to explain," she gasped. "I think this one, he is your spy. I was afraid to bring him here, left him in the bocage. Galopin tied to it. I . . ."

Father Simon raised a hand to stop her. "Go home. Someone else will handle this."

Eponine didn't have to be asked twice. She dashed home. By the time Eponine got there she quaked all over as if chilled. Her words spilled out in teary incoherence. Maman gathered Eponine into her arms and rocked her, just as she had when Eponine was tiny, distraught by some childhood catastrophe. Many times, Eponine remembered being in her mother's embrace because of a skinned knee or the loss of a kite in the park. But this time, she thought, she had reason to cry. This terror was real, and she had left Galopin in the middle of it, then not gone back for him.

It was a cowardly thing to do.

"Hush," Maman murmured. "You did what you had to."

But had she? Had she done anything right at all? She had disobeyed orders and broken her promise. Scenarios spun about her head in a whirlwind of maybes. Maybe she hadn't even heard the man correctly in the first place. Maybe *Scheisse* was both a German and an English word. Maybe the man was just another downed pilot, and Eponine had gotten excited over nothing. Maybe he was a defecting German, doing what her Johannes hoped to do, and she had gotten him into trouble. Maybe he was a spy and had taken Galopin and escaped. Then Gestapo would soon be by to pick them all up. Each possibility seemed more terrible than the last.

Eponine sobbed. "Maybe they'll come for us all now and it will all be my fault."

"If they come, they come," Maman said. "I will stay where they will find me, so they won't search the house thoroughly. Barbe, you go to the mayor's house. Tell René that Eponine is ill and won't go to school. Then go see what you can find out. If it's safe, come back here. If not, it has been good knowing you."

Barbe nodded gravely. She shook Maman's hand. "One way or another we shall all get a cross. Either a medal or a gravestone. Let us pray for the former."

"Bonne chance," Maman said as Barbe slipped out the door into a morning gone pink and orange with sunrise. Eponine knew Barbe would need good luck.

They stayed together as the sun rose and the bright patterns on the floors shortened. Eponine sat curled on her mother's tiny lap. She didn't want to leave the warm comfort of her mother's embrace. Maman smelled like the linen she had slept in, the roasted barley in the ersatz coffee, of chicken feathers and hay from the barn and a million other, earthy scents. She smelled like France as it was in her memory, before the Germans had spread the sharp smells of boot polish and grease, woolen uniforms and sawdust bread. Eponine heard the faint sounds of creatures scuttling in the rafters. She looked up,

"There are the mice again," Eponine said.

"Hush," Maman said, soothing Eponine's hair. "Let's not worry about them right now."

A flock of pigeons whirred past the window, then landed on the barn, where they cooed contentedly. Far away she heard a horse whinny and assumed that it was René's Hortense. Dust motes danced in the sunlight like minuscule fairies. Somewhere a rooster crowed.

"This resistance work: does it frighten you, Maman?"

"It terrifies me," her mother answered.

"Then why do you do it?"

Maman stroked Eponine's hair smooth. "I do it for your father. I want him to be proud of me when he comes back."

"Then, I will do it, too," Eponine said, and felt a little braver. And then Eponine heard the sound she had been waiting for – and dreading – all morning: the sound of an engine.

She tensed and felt her mother's body tense as well. "Can you tell?" she whispered. Maman shook her head no. Her face looked drawn, taut with concentration. And then it relaxed.

"Gasogene," Maman said. "Hear how roughly it runs?"

A little pick-up pulled up in front of the house. Its bed was covered with a tarp on which "*Boucherie Maignart, Caen*" was written in bright red letters. Eponine relaxed. The Gestapo wouldn't arrive in a butcher's delivery truck. A man climbed out of the back and thanked the driver, who had taken a small log from the bag lashed to the running board and was poking it into the fuel compartment.

Eponine recognized the man who entered the door. He was Moreau, the man who had questioned her after her trip to the beach. He looked even shorter and grayer this time, as if the few weeks since they had last met had aged him a decade.

"It's done," he said, dropping his hat onto the kitchen table and collapsing into a chair.

"What is?" Maman asked.

He smiled, bringing Eponine a fresh batch of tears.

"I owe you an apology, ma petite. You are more observant than I had guessed. And you were right about this one."

"Did he get away?" Maman asked.

Moreau shook his head. He reached into the inner pocket of his jacket and brought out a pack of cigarettes. The pack had a red bull's eye on it; an American brand, made with real tobacco. As he breathed out the first puff of smoke, Eponine had a flash of memory. This was the brand her father had smoked.

"The priest called our men," Moreau continued. "They found him exactly where you said he would be. He will bother us no more."

He took a long drag on his cigarette. "We will have to find out where the slip came – how he got into the system in the first place. There may be some treachery to root out further up the line, but for the time being, you are safe."

"Then, it's all right that I talked with this one?" Eponine asked tremulously.

Moreau grinned. "Just don't make a habit of it."

Maman breathed out and Eponine realized that her mother had been holding her breath. "That is good. I didn't know how we would move . . . you know." She jerked her chin upwards.

"It's not something you have to worry about," Moreau said.

"And my horse?" Eponine's heart skipped about.

Moreau smiled. "Your house guest will bring him back later today."

It had been a day of terrible waiting, and she had been as tense as a drawn bow, waiting for the enemy to appear. But now the waiting was over, and with it the need for vigilance. Eponine's body relaxed and her mind went fuzzy. She slid off her mother's lap, climbed the stairs and abandoned herself to a dreamless sleep.

CHAPTER FOURTEEN
MICE

Eponine awoke into soft blue evening twilight. Father Simon sat on the edge of her bed. Anti-aircraft guns thumped in the distance. High up, where the sun still touched the sky, white puffs stood like polka dots on a periwinkle dress.

"Are they bombing the airfield near Caen?" Eponine clutched her stuffed horse to her chest. The cloth was so old and worn that every string showed. She considered hiding it away, but decided that, since Father Simon was a priest, he'd seen worse than a shabby old stuffed horse. He'd seen jealousy and anger and hate and sin.

He laid a hand on her forehead. The priest's fingers felt soft and warm and strong. "You were very brave."

Eponine felt her face flush. "A little girl with her stuffed toy and you call her brave."

"Everyone needs something to comfort them. It looks like that horse has been with you a long time."

"My father gave it to me. He asked me to keep it safe. I've been waiting a long time to show him that I did what he told me to." Eponine turned her eyes from the dotted sky to the priest. In the half-light he looked very young, more brother than father. "You see now that my German soldier wasn't the spy."

"He may still be one," Father Simon said. "Rumor has it that the increased bombings are preparing the way for the invasion. More bombing means more downed crew, which means more work for us. The Germans are desperate to break our organization."

He turned his face at the sound of footfalls as Maman entered. Eponine noticed how thin the priest's hair was becoming. Was this, she wondered, from lack of food or from worry? He was too young to be losing it with age. Maman sat on the other side of the bed. Eponine looked from one face to another and suppressed the blasphemous thought that they made a very nice looking couple. She closed her eyes and pushed the idea away. Appearances could be deceiving. More and more, Eponine understood that nothing in her life was as it seemed. She wasn't a red-headed Breton among the dark, sullen Normans. Her mother wasn't a timid sparrow. Her cousin was no relative at all. Germans were friends; friendly boys could turn her over to the Gestapo. Were all her assumptions untrue?

"I've been thinking, Maman," Eponine said. "This morning you told Barbe you would stay in the open so the Nazis wouldn't search. You must be hiding something – or someone. Those aren't mice in the attic, are they?"

Maman smiled at Father Simon over Eponine's head. It was a sad smile, but proud, acknowledging that if Eponine had lost her innocence, she had also grown wise. "We can't keep anything from this one, can we? She is as sharp as her father. No, ma petite, they aren't mice."

"Who is up there?" Eponine asked. "Radio men transmitting information to England? Spies? Maquisards? Members of the Résistance?"

"See for yourself." Maman took Eponine's hand and led her into the hall. Barbe waited at the top of the stairs, where a small landing wrapped around the brick chimney from the ground floor fireplace. Maman walked around the masonry, to the narrow part of the landing. She picked up the wooden clothes rack that was used as a place to dry clothes when it was too wet outside and passed it over Eponine's head to Father Simon, who set it in the hall. Maman pressed on the wall and a panel popped out with a metallic click. Eponine gasped. She had never realized that there was a space within the wall between her bedroom and the stairs leading down to the main floor, but there it was – a space as wide as the chimney. She looked inside. A steep flight of stairs climbed into the space between the ceiling of her room and the roof of the house. "I never knew we had a room up there," she murmured.

Maman shrugged. "I'd hardly call it a room. It isn't even tall enough to stand up in." She turned her face to the ladder. "Come on down, dears," Maman said. "It's all right now."

"Is it over?" a girl's voice, thin as fog, came down the stairs.

"Can we go home now?" asked another female voice, younger and even thinner.

"No, but it's safe for a while. Come and eat downstairs. Stretch your muscles."

A pair of pale, bare feet appeared on the upper stair. As they moved down, Eponine saw a dusty gray skirt, then a shabby blouse, yellowed and wrinkled with use, then a face that looked like a pale, thin ghost of her friend Sarah Salomon. A younger ghost, whom Eponine would have guessed was Sarah's sister, Ester, followed.

"Sarah? Is that you?" Eponine's voice sounded more like a gasp than a spoken word. She reached out one finger and touched her friend hesitantly, as if she expected her hand to go right through Sarah. But it didn't. In spite of the grayness of her clothing and her skin, Sarah was solid flesh and blood. Eponine poked Sarah again, testing her eyes and her suppositions. Smiling playfully, Sarah poked Eponine back. They fell into each other's arms, laughing. Eponine felt the frailness of her friend's body and the warmth of their friendship.

"You're skin and bones," Eponine said.

"They're wasting away up there," Father Simon said. "No exercise, no fresh air, little food. All they do day and night is lay on cots in the dark and try to be quiet."

"It's very boring," Ester, said.

"Hush," Sarah said. "Don't be ungrateful."

"How do you keep occupied?" Eponine asked. "Do you read?"

Sarah shook her head. "It's too dark, and we don't dare light a lamp. Mostly I do long math problems in my head, or I work on number sequences. I don't mind. I know that everyone is doing what they can."

"I mind," Ester said. Sarah glared at her little sister, who went white and bit her lip.

"I bring them food, but only at night, when you sleep," Maman said.

"She trades us an empty chamber pot for a clean one then, too, so it don't get too stinky up there," Ester added, trying to make up for her previous outburst.

Eponine handed Ester her ratty stuffed horse. "This isn't much, but perhaps it can keep you entertained. When I was little I made mountains and hills with my bed covers, then raced my horse over it."

"What's its name?" Ester pressed the ragged toy to her chest.

"Galopin," Eponine answered.

Ester nodded. "So you don't need this Galopin anymore. You have the new, real Galopin. But don't worry. I'll take good care of this one."

Rage welled up in Eponine's chest. "Have they been here all along? And all the while I was so alone -- without a single friend!"

"This war and its misery isn't all about you," Barbe chided.

"And it's not true you had no friends," Maman added. "You had René."

Sarah lifted an eyebrow at Eponine. A dimple creased her cheek. "René? Ooh, la la. Tell me more about this."

Eponine felt her face flush. She changed the subject. "Where is the rest of your family?"

"Papa and our brother are . . ." Ester began, but Father Simon cut her off.

"Elsewhere. That's all you know, right Ester?"

The little girl shrugged, too embarrassed to answer.

"Are they all here in Amblie, or in Reviers? Or did you have to send them farther away?" Eponine asked.

"How many times do I have to tell you! It's better you don't know," Maman said. "Come, let us eat."

Downstairs they found Barbe Willocque huddled at the table with Moreau, two tumblers and a bottle of wine between them. Barbe looked disheveled, with scratches on her face and twigs in her hair, but her smile beamed triumphantly. Eponine shrieked for joy and hurtled down the stairs and into Barbe's outstretched arms, but only for a moment. Then she sped into the yard. If Madame Willocque was back, that meant Galopin was as well.

Eponine raced to the barn and then hesitated in the doorway. Even in the darkness she sensed that something was wrong. Galopin's discomfort and the sweet scent of blood filled the air.

Galopin threw his head and gave a little whinny of welcome. "Hush," Eponine responded. She stepped forward and embraced his thick neck, leaning her cheek into his and closing her eyes in a little prayer to the God she was beginning to wonder about. When she opened her eyes the stable was lit with the dim yellow light of the kerosene lantern.

"I'm sorry about his legs. I think they will heal, but it will be hard on a horse as old as he." Barbe hung the lantern on a nail.

In the faint light the bandages covering his forelegs looked black with blood. Eponine gasped. "What happened?"

"When he discovered the maquisards upon him, your spy tried to escape on Galopin. Maybe horses can smell Germans. Maybe they have a sixth sense. Galopin fought back valiantly. He threw the man into the bushes then trampled him." Barbe patted Galopin's nose affectionately. "He is a grand old war horse. Who would have thought by looking at him?"

Eponine swallowed hard. "Did he kill the spy?"

"Thank God, no. He's alive enough to give the maquisards plenty of information. Like its owner, your horse is a true hero."

Eponine squeezed Galopin's neck even tighter, but her smile was all for Barbe.

It was a full table that night. Father Simon, the man called Moreau, Sarah and Ester, Barbe, Maman and Eponine all crowded around. Maman added extra water to the pot, and diced the potatoes and onions extra small, but she also added her full weekly wine ration to the soup, so it tasted good and rich. Eponine didn't care that the bread had been sliced so thin that she could see the light of the kerosene lamp through it, or that the tart that Barbe concocted from grape syrup and dried apples tasted more burned than flavorful. What mattered was that they were all there. While Ester played with Pétain under the table, the others talked in suppressed tones about what was happening in the wider world, and how soon the Allies might drive out the Germans. Eponine felt very adult to be part of the discussion. The taste of freedom seemed on the tip of her tongue.

After having been so isolated in the dark attic, Sarah was anxious to hear the news. But as the evening wore on, her interests went from politics and news of the war to gossip about her classmates. By the time the group broke up, Eponine and Sarah were giggling in each other's arms. The war and all its horrors seemed very distant.

It was well past curfew when the men slipped into the darkness and made their way back to the rectory. Eponine felt the weight of the world come back to her with each step up the stairs. She hugged Sarah, then Sarah and her sister slipped behind the panel and disappeared.

CHAPTER FIFTEEN
LABELS

Eponine slid between the cold linen sheets. The crickets outside her bedroom window sounded so peaceful, so normal, but Eponine knew the world outside was neither peaceful nor normal. People were suffering: some in isolation like the friend immediately above her, others in camps like the one Barbe Willocque had described. Not that long ago she had felt the most ill-used person in the whole world just because Marie and Marthe Boivin spoke unkindly to her and the other girls on the playground excluded her. The thought made her blush with shame. She crossed her arms behind her head. How little her problems seemed compared to others.

After a while, Maman came in and sat on the edge of Eponine's bed for the second time that day.

"Is my father squirreled away in an attic somewhere like Sarah?"

"Perhaps," Maman said, "though I doubt it. Your father was never one to sit on his hands when there was work to be done."

"You don't know where he is, do you?"

Maman shrugged. "Perhaps he is in Poland, helping the Jews. Or in the jungles of Dutch East India. He could be ferrying refugees over the Himalayas, out of Mongolia. Maybe he went back to America and he'll return with the invasion forces. One never knows with your father. He is always going here and there to help a worthy cause. That's why we saw so little of him when you were young."

Eponine sighed. "You told me he built bridges."

"Oh, he does," Maman said. "Bridges over cultural barriers. Bridges to freedom and democracy for people everywhere."

Eponine tried another tack. "Where was he when last you heard from him?"

"Spain," Maman said. "He might be there still."

"Helping allied fliers get to Gibraltar?"

Maman shook her head. "Remember how I told you that your father fought for France before the United States entered the Great War? Well, he did the same thing when the United States refused to intervene against Franco. He joined a band of Americans called the Abraham Lincoln Battalion. They fought for the Spanish Republic."

Eponine rubbed her forehead. Maman was talking about something that happened a long time ago, before the Germans came to France. "Maman, are you talking about the Spanish Civil War?"

"Of course," Maman said.

"Is that why we came here? Because Papa was fighting against Franco?"

"Oh, no," Maman said. "We came here before that, when he went to Ethiopia to fight Mussolini. Don't you remember taking the train back to Paris to meet him? We had three glorious days with him before he left for Spain."

Eponine shook her head. If she remembered anything of those three days they were jumbled up with earlier memories. "So, Papa went to Spain and we never heard from him again?"

Maman nodded. "We heard for a while. Letters. An occasional package. And then there was an ambush on the Ebro River. The men were scattered through the hills. Drowned. Lost. That was in the spring of '37."

"And you haven't heard from him since?"

"That doesn't mean he's dead." Maman became more agitated with each passing word. Her hands twined and untwined, her fingers interlacing like a basket of snakes. Every few moments she shook them loose as if they were tingling, but they immediately found solace in entanglement again. She rocked, her body swaying back and forth, rhythmically lulling herself into peace. "Your father wasn't the kind to give up without a fight. One look at his face would tell you that. Most men who had been burned like he had wouldn't have survived. He has found another fight elsewhere – other people who need his help."

Eponine gave her mother a goodnight kiss. She put her arms behind her head and stared at the ceiling. For years she had been sure that her father would return and set everything to rights. Now she was sure that Karadoc Lambaol, or whatever the red headed man with the fiery green eyes set into a charred and warped face was called, wasn't building bridges. He was in heaven, wherever that was, with his God, who ever that was. Karadoc Lambaol wasn't going to come back and restore Eponine's happiness. He wasn't going to whisk her away from the nasty, provincial Normans. He wasn't going to throw the Germans out of France. He wasn't going to move her family back to Paris, to the blissful life she remembered. The only person who could fix Eponine's world was Eponine.

But who was she? Eponine Lambaol was still not sure.

The clock on the mantel ticked off the minutes through the darkness. Eponine heard it chime ten, then eleven, then midnight, but sleep eluded her. Finally Eponine slipped out of bed and into her worn slippers. She padded into her mother's room. One lump, a small one curled into an impossibly small ball, told Eponine that Barbe wasn't sleeping either. She crept downstairs into the darkened kitchen.

"Barbe?" Eponine whispered.

There was a rustling movement, a wheezy breath. "Here. Careful. Don't trip."

Eponine groped about and found a kitchen chair. She dropped into it with a sigh. "I couldn't sleep."

"Neither could I," Barbe said. "Sometimes memories are waking nightmares. They keep me awake, afraid of what I might see if I dream."

"Tell me about it," Eponine said.

"I've told you once before. Someday when the sun shines and I have no more fear of such places. Then I will tell you, not now."

Eponine rubbed her face with her hand. "I keep thinking. All this time I've been waiting for my father to come back and rescue my mother and me. Now I realize that I can't count on him. I need to take care of myself. But how can I when I don't even know who I am?"

"You know who you are," Barbe said.

"No I don't. I thought I was a Breton named Eponine Lambaol. Now I learn I'm an Irish American French girl with an alias."

"So you do know who you are. And you know what great bravery and intelligence you are capable of. All you don't know is your name. What, after all, is a name? A few syllables your parents gave you at birth? A label? Be who you are – who you already know yourself to be and forget all the labels that others have put on you. Then you will know how to live. Now go to bed and try to get some sleep."

A divide exists between the heart and the head. From it speaks the still, small voice that whispers hope to the heart even when the head rationally knows that defeat and hopelessness are inevitable. Its words bubble up fresh and clear as water from a spring. It quenches desiccated dreams. If the heart listens, that voice gains power until it rumbles like a mighty torrent, loud enough to drown out both the head's reason and the world's opposition.

Jeanne d'Arc listened to that still, small voice and she saved a nation.

After her talk with Maman, Eponine had been convinced that the only rational explanation for his long absence was that her father was dead. But a trickle of hope seeped into her heart with the morning light. The tiny stream bubbled and babbled throughout the school day. Perhaps her father wasn't dead. Perhaps, if she lived bravely, like Barbe suggested, when he came back he would be proud of her. It occurred to her that her mother lived with the same hope. That hope preoccupied Eponine so much that she didn't hear her teachers' lectures. She did not taste her meager lunch, nor see the shy, tentative smile René offered her over the lunch table.

"I missed you yesterday," René said as he trailed along behind Eponine on their way home. "The school seemed empty without you."

Eponine shrugged. "Lots of students miss. Hunger sickness is finally getting to all of us."

René glanced at a sky yellowed with heat and dust. It hadn't rained in days. The fields were parched. The distant drone of British bombers, punctuated by the heavy guns along the coast, filled the air. "We can't feed our people because the Allies destroy supply lines."

"And because of German requisitions?" Eponine teased.

"They wouldn't requisition so much if they didn't have to fight so hard. The British and their allies prolong the war. That's why we're starving."

"I'm glad you understand it all," Eponine said, sure he would miss her sarcasm. "The rest of us are so bewildered by all the differing reports that we can't think straight."

"It's hunger sickness that's befuddling you, not the news. Come to the Mairie on Sunday for dinner. After, we listen to '*l'Alphabet de la famille*' on the radio. It's a wise program, and very entertaining."

Eponine shook her head. "Sunday dinner is family time."

"You mean your Maman and that house guest? My Papa says that is hardly what he calls a family."

Eponine felt her face flush with outrage but she held her tongue. If the mayor was insinuating the same lewd possibility as the Boivin sisters, let him think so. As Barbe had said, it blinded him to other possibilities. "It's not my fault that Papa must build bridges."

"We wouldn't have mandatory service if the British didn't destroy our bridges as fast as we repair them. But back to Sunday: I have something important to show you. Please come."

"I will think about it." Eponine clamped her mouth shut. If René was trying to make up for accosting her, his incendiary remarks about her family certainly weren't helping his cause. Still, Maman and Barbe both wanted Eponine to patch up her relationship with René.

Eponine was still thinking about her father when she went back to Reviers to get the day's supply of bread and milk later that afternoon.

"What are you doing here?" she asked when she met Father Simon in the street, a string bag in his hand.

Father Simon opened the door to the butcher's shop and allowed

Eponine to go in first. "Even priests don't live on the Word alone. We must buy supplies just like everyone else. You didn't expect Madame Tournebulle to bear the burden of shopping as well as of cooking and cleaning, did you?"

"I suppose not," she said. That priests needed to buy groceries had never occurred to her. She realized that her teachers also had separate lives, homes and families separate from school. Did any of them lead secret lives, hiding away downed airmen or feeding the maquisards like she and her mother and this priest?

"Father, is the same heaven for Protestants and Catholics? How does one get there? Why can't God just stop this war and let us have heaven here instead of waiting for it?"

"These are big questions." Father Simon said.

The butcher, Monsieur Du Gouey, leaned his forearms against his cabinet and smiled at the priest. "Maybe that is why God allows war — to make our young people think about Him."

Father Simon shrugged. "I can think of less severe measures he could have taken." He turned to Eponine. "Come to the church one afternoon. Or we could walk in the fields and talk."

"I would like that very much." Eponine handed over her ration coupons and a wad of francs. Monsieur Du Gouey passed back a parcel wrapped in white butcher's paper, then a handful of small coins.

He winked. "I've added in two extra slices of cold cuts. I know you can use them."

Eponine felt her face redden. Did Monsieur Du Gouey know about the mice in her attic, or was he just being nice? She thought of all the times he'd thrown in a couple of extra sausages, an extra quarter pound of pork. Surely he was part of the Résistance, but she dare not ask.

Eponine went to the Boivin Sisters' bakery, where she traded her coupons and money for three small loaves of dark brown bread and a handful of spiteful insults. Maybe Marie and Marthe Boivin did not sympathize with the Germans, but they surely weren't on her side of this war. She emerged from the bakery and found Johannes Hegel by Galopin. The undamaged side of his face wrinkled in concern.

"Bonjour, Jeanne. Galopin looks injured.. Are you all right?"

Eponine averted her eyes. The concern in his voice made her feel terrible. If her father was alive, he was off fighting for a dream instead of taking care of his family. Her father was very different from this sergeant, who wanted nothing more than to never fight again. He couldn't be a spy. Or could he? Eponine couldn't be sure. All these people — all these labels — and Eponine didn't know which to believe and which not to. Tears burned in the corners of her eyes.

"Pardon me, monsieur. I can't talk to you anymore," she mumbled at her toes.

A look of deep sadness took the place of concern on his face. "I understand. I'm, after all, German. Good day to you, and much happiness after the war."

Eponine swung onto Galopin's back. As she passed the butcher's shop, she saw two faces pressed against the window, watching her. She nodded to Father Simon and Monsieur Du Gouey and solemnly rode home.

CHAPTER SIXTEEN
SUNDAY DINNER

Maman insisted that Eponine wear her best dress on Sunday. After all, she was going to the Mairie, which was practically like being invited to a state dinner. Maman fussed to make sure the lace collar hung just so around her neck, and that her shoes, though tight, were shiny. She brushed Eponine's auburn hair to a lustrous glow, then rolled it tightly and pinned it in place. The effect took Eponine's breath away and brought crimson to her cheeks. She didn't look like a scrawny girl with her hair done up, but, in spite of her diminutive size, a very mature, red haired version of her mother.

Barbe Willocque glanced up from her book as Eponine walked down the stairs. "Ah, the mayor will be pleased. You are the embodiment of the kind of woman the Vichy government wants: clean and neat, beautiful and modest. Just the type to raise the spirits of our men and guide us into a new era of morality and family life."

"Don't tease me," Eponine said, glad that she had talked her mother out of rouge and lipstick. "You sound just like René."

"I'm not teasing! I sound like René because I'm looking at you through his expectations – and his father's. Be clever. Use this opportunity to get on the mayor's good side. The more he likes you, the less he will think that you are involved in anything – bad." The face she made as she said the last word made Eponine laugh.

Halfway down rue l'Eglise, Hortense nickered and trotted over to the fence. The horse looked immense, her flanks as round as a barrel. Afraid she might sully her dress, Eponine resisted the urge to slip through the fence and run her hands over the bulge, feeling for the foal within. She sauntered the rest of the way, very pleased with herself. She imagined the look on René's face when he saw her.

The look she imagined wasn't a thing like the horror and disbelief that crossed her face when she saw René Bonté standing at attention on the Mairie's door sill. But for the blue beret and a blue patch on his chest, he looked like a German soldier. Eponine held a hand to her mouth to suppress her scream.

"Surprised?" His eyes scanned her hair, her dress, the shine of her shoes and his eyebrows shot up. "My, you look beautiful."

"What are you wearing?" Eponine squeaked out the question.

"My new uniform. I'm going to prove my valor to you. I have *joined la Légion des Volontaires Français Contre le Bolchevisme.*"

"The Legion of French Volunteers against Bolshevism? Oh, René! You didn't join because of me?" she asked.

"Precisely because of you. I will fight alongside the Germans on the Eastern Front."

"You're too young!"

René puffed out his chest, reminding Eponine of a preening pigeon. "That's one of the benefits of being the mayor's son. My Papa got a special waiver so that I could join early. I'm very lucky, non?"

Tears welled in Eponine's eyes. Whether or not the official news listened to in the Bonté house said so, Radio Free London said that the Eastern Front had collapsed into disarray. René would be nothing but idealistic cannon fodder, a screen for the retreating Germans. "Oh, René, I'm so sorry. You shouldn't have done this for me."

"I leave tomorrow. Perhaps, after dinner, you will give me a hero's leave?" René blushed so brightly that Eponine felt her face go scarlet, too, but she couldn't answer. He led her through the ground floor, which was taken up by the mayor's office and meeting and assembly rooms, then up a flight of stairs to the family's private apartments. Eponine repressed the sense that she was intruding. She had, after all, been invited.

The mayor, enthroned in a dark leather reading chair, looked up over the top of his half-moon glasses at her and smiled benignly. "Ah! A future constituent! Come in! Come in, ma petite. Hermione! René's little guest is here." He shouted this last bit over his shoulder to a door which must have led to the kitchen, for a rather plump woman with an apron stretched taut around her very ample waist appeared there, wooden spoon in hand.

"Very good," she said, fingering the pearls that just peeked out between the top of the apron and the lowest roll of her chin. "Supper will be on the table shortly. Do have a seat."

Eponine looked around at the cozy room. A settee and two luxurious chairs sat by the bay window. On the opposite wall was a door that led into the dining room, where Eponine could see the table set with china and silver. It looked very opulent, especially compared with her house, where one room served as kitchen, living room and dining room. A record of an upbeat song by Charles Trenet played on the wind-up gramophone.

René guided her to the settee. They sat side by side and looked through an enormous book of black and white photographs of Paris from before the war. After a few minutes, René's older brother Jacques slunk into the room and threw himself into a chair by the window.

"I'm home," he shouted toward the kitchen. "You may serve now."

"Very funny," Madame Bonte said, but Eponine could tell by the humor in her voice that she did, indeed find it funny. At the very least, she indulged him. Jacques pulled a couple of dried leaves off the front of his khaki shirt and crumbled them onto the floor. He straightened his black tie and glared at the leaves. "Don't you ever dust in here? This place is a mess!"

"Sorry," Madame Bonte called cheerfully. "It's hard, since we let the servants go. But wartime requires sacrifices of all of us. Time to eat! Come to the table!"

"May I help carry out the dishes?" Eponine scurried to the kitchen door.

Madame scowled at her good naturedly. "Most assuredly not! You are our guest. Now, go sit down so I may serve the soup." She jerked her chin toward the dining room and Eponine hurried in and sat while René held out her chair for her. Soon all except the Mayor himself sat around a table filled with steaming soup bowls and baskets of rich rolls. The mayor set the tips of his fingers on each side of his plate and leaned forward as if beginning a long speech.

"Are they not a handsome set, my two boys?" he asked Eponine.

"Oh, yes, Monsieur," she answered.

"And quite patriotic?"

"Quite," Eponine agreed, although she would have argued if asked the same question anywhere else.

"Have we forgotten something?"

Eponine quickly folded her hands, anticipating a prayer for the meal, but instead, the family put their hands over their hearts and recited:

"Monsieur le Maréchal, I firmly believe in all the truths you teach, because you can't err or deceive the people."

The mayor smiled at Eponine, who sat with her mouth agape. "That is the act of faith composed by the newspaper *Le Franciste* for our new messiah. And now, Jacques, the oath of allegiance to the *Milice Française?*"

Jacques dragged himself reluctantly to his feet. He stuck out his arm in the Nazi salute. "I swear to fight against democracy, against Gaullist insurrections and against the Jewish leprosy. There. We can eat now, before the food gets cold."

The dinner which came after the soup was very grand and there was lots of it. She nearly swallowed whole the chicken breast baked in white wine sauce. She ate every one of her tiny spring peas and potatoes, every last leaf of lettuce in her salad. But she didn't enjoy them. The fat, buttery rolls tasted bitter in her mouth when she thought of the dark, hard bread that Maman and Barbe were eating with their thin soup. There would be no second course in the Lambaol house.

Jacques' fork clattered to his plate. "This chicken is inedible. The bird must have been as old as Pétain himself."

"Hush," Madame Bonté said. "Don't be disrespectful of the man who is going to save France. And remember to be grateful that you have chicken at all. There is, after all, a war going on."

"No one could eat this. Look how stringy it is!" Jacques gestured with both hands. Eponine fought the urge to ask if she could take it home with her. She hadn't seen that much meat in a month. It was a terrible sin to waste it.

"How went the *shanghaillage* this afternoon?" the Mayor asked.

Eponine dropped her fork, attracting more attention than she wanted. "*Shanghaillage?* What is that, if you please?" Whatever it was, it had a bad sound to it.

"The work of the *Comité Pour la Paix Sociale*," Jacques explained. "I work for them part time, when I'm not busy on Milice business. I receive a salary and a small bounty for each man I bring in."

"Bring in?" Eponine asked, not sure she wanted to know.

Jacques rolled his eyes at her denseness. "Press into factory service."

"Oh," Eponine felt her skin crawl. She knew that men were kidnapped out of movie lines and restaurant seats and sent to munitions factories far away, but she had always assumed that the Germans were to blame for this atrocity. She couldn't imagine Jacques doing so. Yet neither he nor his family seemed to think there was anything wrong with it.

Madame Bonté leaned her copious bosom over her soup, endangering the flower pinned to her lace collar. "Surely you've heard of such things, my dear?"

Eponine stared at her soup, unsure what to say.

"Ah, she is such an innocent," Madame said with a sigh. "Hurry with your meat, René, or we won't be finished before the others come."

"The others?" Eponine asked.

"The whole neighborhood comes by to listen to the news every evening," René said.

Jacques leaned forward and smiled in a rather ugly way. "Except for a few holdouts – social isolates who don't bother to mix with the rest of us."

Eponine averted her eyes, knowing full well that he meant her family.

As others arrived, the Bontés left the dishes at the table and retired to the living room. Eponine recognized perhaps two dozen people, mostly farmers and out of work businessmen, seated on the dining room chairs or lounging against the walls. Madame Bonté took the majority of the settee. René crushed into one edge of the seat and Eponine sat on the other side. She clung to the arm to keep herself from listing into Madame. Eponine squirmed, uneasy both because the fit was so tight on the settee and because she was increasingly aware of how different she felt about what was going on in the world. According to Barbe Willocque, *L'Alphabet de la Famille* broadcast what Maréchal Pétain's Vichy government wanted people to believe was the average French family. On the show a mother, father, son, daughter, grandfather and uncle all continued their sunny domestic life as though times in France were normal. Before radios became illegal, her mother had laughed at the show. This family took it seriously.

The Mayor shook everyone's hand and engaged in a few pleasantries and a brief welcome speech, then returned to his paper. Jacques lounged lazily, swinging his leg over the side of the chair as he watched her with a bored look. The farmers stared with vacant eyes. Out of work shopkeepers shuffled with tense unease. Eponine felt herself growing uneasy. Surely this was a trap to catch her leftist leanings.

The radio program went through the alphabet, the letters representing the patriotic and family values that Pétain espoused: a for *amour* or love, b for *bonté*, or goodness.

"That's us," René whispered over his mother's stomach, a wide grin on his face. C for comprehension, d for devotion. Cold sweat broke out on Eponine's forehead. She feared she might embarrass herself and throw up Madame Bonté's dinner. She thought her ears were buzzing with stress until the big guns on the shore boomed and she realized that what she heard was the sound of distant bombers. Monsieur le Maire looked up from his paper.

"Even on Sunday," he muttered. "It just proves they aren't good Christians."

The sound grew louder. It drowned out the radio. Madame Bonté waved her hand dismissively. "René, love, might as well turn it off." The light flickered as if clouds were passing over the sun. The bombers were coming in from the west. The roar rattled in Eponine's chest, pulling the wind from her lungs. She fought the urge to scream.

Madame Bonté was heaving herself off the settee when Eponine heard another, higher pitched whine grow out of the low rumble of the bombers. "Only a Focke-Wulf 190 makes a sound like that! It's the Abbeville kids," Jacques leaped out of his seat and began a stampede of farmers toward the door.

"The what?" Eponine shouted into René's ear.

"The Abbeville kids! Goering's most elite fighter squadron. They fly Focke-Wulf 190s, fast little planes that are deadly against lumbering bombers." René grabbed Eponine's hand and pulled her down the stairs. The sound built to a deafening climax as fighter planes sped overhead, then dropped away in both pitch and volume as they sped northward, towards the coast.

"Shouldn't we stay where it's safe?" she yelled. Hermann Goering was the Air Marshal for the entire German Luftwaffe. Going outside while his deadliest planes shot down massive bombers sounded like suicide.

"And miss the show? No, thank you," René shouted back. Hand in hand they ran through the public rooms and into the crossroads, joining other villagers around the beehive well.

Eponine shaded her eyes with her hand as the first bomber passed directly overhead. The planes were enormous, and low enough that she could see the markings on their wings and the painted ladies on their noses. They flew in such tight formation that she feared they would touch wings and plummet to earth, right where she stood.

"There," Jacques pointed north, where one bomber seemed to lag behind the others, cut out from the formation like a wounded animal trailing behind the herd. It was flying lower, a cloud of yellow-nosed Focke-Wulf 190s buzzing around it like angry bees. Eponine couldn't hear the roar of the 20 mm cannons over the drone of the bombers, but she saw bright flashes of light coming from the German fighters. The bomber was taking on plenty of lead. Black smoke billowed from one of the engines. The blur of the propeller slowed. The behemoth plane bucked and shuddered. What kept it afloat? Just after it passed Amblie a string of white parachutes appeared beneath the doomed plane and floated gently to earth. Men, tiny as ants, hung beneath each one. Eponine counted five. How many men made up a crew on such an enormous plane? More smoke poured from the bomber as it listed onto its side and veered west, disappearing into the trees. An enormous explosion shook the earth, then silence so profound that Eponine heard her heart beating in her throat. The villagers, knowing the show was over, made for their homes.

"Well," Madame Bonté said, "That was nice. Now let's have our dessert."

"Did you feel the earth shudder when the bomber crashed?" René asked.

"I wonder what happened to the crew," Eponine said.

"The plane was too low when they bailed," Jacques said with a sneer. "They probably splattered like ripe melons. Our Milice will pick up the survivors."

Eponine shuddered. Please, God, she thought, if you are listening, don't let the Milice get those men. Guide them to me and let me help.

Dessert consisted of real coffee, with thick, rich cream and Madeleine cookies made with real butter, but the excited talk about the German fighters ruined the food for Eponine. The madeleines' scalloped ridges looked too much like parachutes. Jacques and René made them sound brave, but to Eponine the Fock-Wulf 190s reminded her of her headmaster, Monsieur Couturier's, vivid description of the jackals harrying a wounded elephant. The German fighters were shameful little bullies, not heroes.

Jacques leaned forward and grinned wolfishly at Eponine. "You've been very quiet all through dessert."

Eponine stared at the crumbled cookies on her plate. "Seeing that plane go down was emotional."

"It's almost as if you were cheering for the British," Jacques said. "Where do your sympathies lie? To prove your loyalty, I think you should be an *indic.*"

Eponine's heart clenched but she said nothing. What would he do to force her to be an informer? Hold her under house arrest here in the Mairie? Turn her over to the Gestapo?

"Go ahead," Jacques needled. "Tell us something about a neighbor or a school mate. Something of interest to the Milice."

"But monsieur, I have nothing to report." Before she could stop herself Eponine burst into sobs.

"Oh, look," Madame chided. "You've frightened her. She is such an innocent, Jacques, so naive. How would such a tiny little sparrow of a girl know anything of value?"

"I was only joking." Jacques picked crumbs off his jacket.

"It wasn't very nice," René said. "Now look what you've done. Ruined a perfectly lovely Sunday dinner." He placed a gentle hand on Eponine's shoulder. "I'm sorry. Come, let me walk you home."

Once they were outside, René tried to put his arm around Eponine's shoulders. She pulled away and wrapped her arms over her chest, hugging herself tightly. She hiccupped repeatedly. A tiny little sparrow of a girl, René's mother had called her. Right now she did feel small and vulnerable.

René stopped her in front of her own doorway. He placed his hands on her shoulders and gently turned her around. "I'm sorry that Jacques teased you so mercilessly, ma petite rousette. Maman was right. You really are an innocent; so sweet, so childlike, so innocent, so virginal, so . . . ."

Eponine turned her head away. "Stop it," she said through clamped lips.

"This isn't how I envisioned our last moment together." He sighed. "Won't you give me a goodbye kiss?"

Eponine did not respond.

"Will you wait for me? You won't get another boyfriend when I'm gone?"

"Of course not, René." She wiped a tear off her cheek with the back of her hand. This much she could promise. Who else, after all, was there? In

Eponine's experience there wasn't a single other boy in all of Normandy who would give a second glance to a girl with red hair and freckles. Whether she was Breton or American-Irish didn't matter; she was still foreign and strange.

Eponine felt René's grip on her shoulders relax. "If I don't come back, I want you to have Hortense's foal."

"You can't do that," Eponine said. "That foal is too valuable."

"My father won't be happy. He's already planned what he will buy with the money she would bring. But Hortense is mine, and the foal is mine to give as I wish. My father won't deny me my dying wish."

Eponine burst into tears. "Don't say that," she burbled through her sobs.

René planted a slow, sweet kiss on her forehead. He took a step back and gave her a stiff-armed salute. And then he was gone.

CHAPTER SEVENTEEN
PERFECT DAY FOR AN INVASION

While Monsieur Auber droned on about the differences between classical and Medieval Latin, Eponine stared out the classroom's open window at the brittle, dry sky. A bead of sweat slipped down her spine, pooling in her sodden waistband. It was the 29th of May, and summer vacation was still six weeks away. Unless they sweltered to death first.

But maybe the Allies would come today and not only liberate France from the Germans, but students from their classes. It was a perfect day for an invasion.

Eponine mopped the back of her neck with her handkerchief. Monsieur Auber's voice was almost as boring, almost as monotonous as the drone of distant bombers. Maybe René had been right. Maybe she should have studied German. It might be the language of the oppressor, but it certainly could be no more oppressive to learn than Latin.

She missed René. The clock's minute hand trembled, then dropped to the next mark on the giant, yellowed face that hung just over the cloudy blackboard. René had left only seven hours ago. It seemed months. Eponine felt another drop of sweat break loose from her collar bone and slither down her chest. The clock hand trembled, then clicked downward again. Another minute, gone.

That morning she was watering Galopin in the cowshed when the deep rumble of a gasoline-powered automobile immobilized her, the empty water bucket suspended above the trough as the last few drops marked time, making round ripples in the horse trough. Gasoline meant German, and a German presence in this village was rare. She stuck her head out the door as a green Citroen, the kind of car that everyone in the schoolyard swore the Gestapo preferred, passed her house and turned at the crossroads. The engine cut off.

Eponine slipped down the shady lane, hugging the wall with her shoulder. At the corner, she peeked over the top edge of the wall. René, in his new uniform, came out of the Mairie. A suitcase dangled from one fist, a sheaf of papers from the other. René threw his things into the Citroen's trunk. He gave his tearful mother a hug and several kisses on both cheeks. He shook his father's hand, and then waved at Jacques, who leaned indolently against the side of the building, looking rather pleased to be losing his only sibling. Eponine ducked her head and scurried back up the lane. After a short while the Citroen's engine roared back to life and she knew that he was on his way to Caen to board the train.

Eponine glanced back at the clock on the classroom wall. The stodgy hour hand indicated that if René was going to Paris he would be there by now, assuming the tracks weren't damaged. Before the war, it had taken only two hours to ride from Caen to Paris. Now it could take up to seven or eight. Sometimes it was impossible. Had René continued beyond Paris? Maybe he was on his way to Berlin, or directly to the front, wherever that was now. Eponine wished she had asked him where exactly he was going, and for how long he would train. Then she wouldn't have to worry about him right away. The strange names she had heard on the BBC flitted through her head. Places like Ploesti and Minsk and Lwow were suddenly interesting, even though she didn't know where they were. She must ask Monsieur Couturier to point them out on the enormous map in the geography class.

That she might have driven him to his death niggled at her conscience, as constant as the drone of the bombers. The clock's minute hand trembled, then dropped another notch, pointing straight down. A moment later the bell for morning recess rang. Eponine slowly pushed out of her seat and ambled to the school yard. With René gone, she had no one to talk to. An insurmountable distrust yawned between Eponine and her classmates. Eponine hesitantly whistled a few bars of Le Chant des Partisans, the song which always closed the Free French Radio program on the BBC. She glanced around, hoping for a sympathetic look. Sophie Junot scowled at her. Every face in the crowd of girls that crowded around Sophie like handmaids to the queen mimicked Sophie's scowl.

"What are you doing, whistling that song?" Sophie's words flew from her lips like shrapnel. Eponine felt her face twitch with their impact. She fought the urge to turn and run.

"Nothing," she said in a whisper.

"As if she could be a resistant. She's not even French," one of the girls muttered to the general assent of the others.

"Maybe she's an indic," Sophie said. "She passes information to that German with the hideous face. She's whistling to make someone implicate himself so she can turn him in. Well, it won't be us." Sophie tipped her nose skyward and spun on her heel. The entire crowd imitated her gesture. They trooped to the other side of the playground. As she passed Eugene and his gang of surly boys, Sophie muttered something. Eugene's eyebrows flew up.

"Eponine's an *indic*, Eponine's an *indic*," Eugene chanted. Soon all the boys joined in.

"What a bunch of monkeys," Eponine thought as she stomped away, her fists tight to her sides. But her heart thudded in her ears. She would have to be careful. Even monkeys could whisper the wrong word into the wrong ear. Then not only she, but the Salomon girls, her mother and Barbe Willocque would all be in trouble.

After school she trudged home beneath a cloudless sky so dry that it appeared bleached, as if the blue had been burned out of it by the heat. The schoolyard chant echoed in her mind. Eponine's an indic, Eponine's an indic. She drove it from her mind and, instead, imagined Rommel, desperately driving his tanks across the scorching sands of Africa with the Desert Rats hot behind him. She gloated over his desperation, felt the parch in his throat and she smiled as if she, herself had caused his defeat. If the Allies wanted to beat Rommel again, this time in Normandy where he was guarding the Atlantic Wall, they had perfect weather for it. Let them come and stop the Germans before either René made it to the front or her classmate's taunts attracted the wrong attention. Let the Allies come today.

She found the house empty, so she dropped her schoolbooks on the kitchen table and went to look for Maman and Barbe. She passed the cow pasture where Galopin, its lone inhabitant, grazed lazily on the fresh, green grass, then found the women bent over a freshly turned row. Pétain, lying on his side nearby, didn't notice her. Barbe's faded trousers and stretched-out sweater made her look like a big-boned man. Her short hair poked out at odd angles through the holes in her straw hat. But Maman wore a skirt and jacket and her twist of dark brown hair shone in the sun like a chestnut's glossy shell. The only thing inelegant about her was the dirt under her nails and the clunky clogs on her feet.

"They're calling me an *indic* in the schoolyard."

Barbe sat back on her heels and wiped her forehead with her handkerchief. "Let them think what they will. It will blind them to other possibilities."

Eponine had heard that before, but it gave her no comfort. She turned her attention to her mother. "Maman, your nice things wouldn't wear out so quickly if you wore old clothes to work in the fields."

"I don't want your father to come home and catch me in rags." Jacquelle

Lambaol replied without looking up. "I want him to be proud of me and how I've held everything together. It would humiliate him to think I've been deprived in his absence."

Eponine bit her lips to keep from saying that if Papa was coming back he would have done so long ago. If he did come home, she was certain to complain long and hard about the length of his absence and the terrible suffering they had endured.

"Perfect day for an invasion," Eponine said instead.

Maman glanced up at the sky. "Perfect day for planting beans. Here. Go down that row a bit before you begin." She poured a handful of seeds into Eponine's hand before she went back to her own work. Eponine moved over one row and began. The soil glistened deep ochre. She took in a deep breath of the chalky smell that made spring so fresh. Were it not for the distant buzzing and the occasional boom of the big guns, she might have forgotten the war.

She passed Father Simon on the road to Reviers when she went for the evening's bread later that afternoon. "Perfect day for an invasion," Eponine said.

The priest looked heavenward and nodded, a smile warming his face.

Instead of going directly home once she had her supplies, Eponine circled south, looking for signs of the downed bomber. She didn't find the plane, but she did find one of the parachutes half exposed in a ditch. Eponine looked around for the pilot, but he was nowhere to be seen. If she couldn't help the pilot, at least she could help Maman. She, like every other woman in France, had been deprived of fabric for too long. Several of the girls in school wore blouses made of parachute fabric. Eponine hauled the fabric from the water, squeezed it as dry as she could, and draped it over Galopin's rump.

"Look what I found," she announced when she returned home, holding up the fabric proudly.

Maman stood up, wincing as she placed her hand on the small of her back. One look at the parachute and she blanched. "Get rid of it."

Eponine gasped. "But why?"

"Dangerous to have," Barbe said, suppressing a cough. "Exposes us to suspicion. People will wonder how we got it."

"We got it by hauling it out of a ditch," Eponine said indignantly. "All the girls in school are wearing blouses made from parachute cloth. It's the new fashion."

"Not for us," Maman wrung her hands. "Do you want people questioning us? René's not around to protect us anymore. Burn it."

"Can't," Barbe said. "It's nylon. Puts off a terrible, recognizable stench when burned. Leaves a nasty black residue that will be even more suspicious than using the fabric. But it can serve us still." Barbe jutted her chin toward the roof of the house and Eponine understood. The fabric could keep the Salomon girls occupied.

Even though there were several hours of daylight left, they left the fields about eight in the evening. Eponine made sure that all the doors and windows were securely locked while Maman and Barbe hung up the blackout blankets. They shared a light supper of cold cuts, hard old raisins, and stale bread with Sarah and Ester. Because the power was out, they washed up by kerosene lantern light.

"Ready?" Barbe asked. Maman nodded and the five of them sneaked down the stairs to the coal cellar to listen to the radio.

Maman pulled the radio from the rags. She checked the connections to the battery, then flipped the switch and carefully scanned the frequencies. The radio whined and hummed until Maman found the exact place. They listened intently, hunched over the little set as first the familiar notes from Beethoven, then the news came over the cracking and popping that Eponine had learned were German attempts at jamming the frequency. Much of the news was about the Allied progress in Italy, but then the announcer said something that made Eponine's spine tingle.

"French residents living along the coast. You are urged to abandon your homes temporarily and move far inland to a safe place. Repeat, you are urged. . . ."

"Hear that?" Eponine hissed. Barbe put a quick finger to her mouth and Maman said "hush," so Eponine settled back in and listened to the announcements about blue cows and the size of cheese wheels. Neither Barbe nor Maman shot a significant glance at the other. Neither twitched. At the end of the program, Maman sighed as she shut off the radio and stuffed it deep in the rag barrel.

"So?" asked Eponine. "What do we do?"

"Nothing," Barbe answered.

"Nothing? Shouldn't we move inland?"

"And leave us to starve?" Ester cried.

"Hush," Sarah said. "No one's going to abandon us."

Maman snorted. "We are inland, darling, or hadn't you noticed?"

"Just a few miles," Eponine said. "Shouldn't we . . ."

"We should put Sarah and Ester back in the attic, then go to bed is what we should do," Maman said. "The invasion won't be here. It will be to the north of us, near Calais or Dunkirk."

"Why?" Eponine asked.

"Think about it. That's where the invasions always come." Maman said.

"But Rommel fortified Courseulles. I saw it."

Barbe snorted. "What you saw was puny compared to what Rommel put in north of us. Our fortifications keep the Allies from outflanking the front."

"Are you sure?" Eponine asked. Both Maman and Barbe shot her looks that made her stop asking questions. Did they know something that she didn't? Had one of the crazy messages on the BBC told them where the Allies were going to land? Or had a maquisard told them?

She spent an hour in the attic with the Salomon girls, chatting about the weather and the news. By the time she went to her own room twilight was over and the sky spangled with stars.

Eponine lay in bed and listened to the crickets and the rustling of small creatures in the hedges. No planes buzzed overhead, no distant thunder came from the guns. It seemed a very anticlimactic end to a day so full of portents.

The sun rose hot the next day, and the papers were full of stories of French cities being bombed, but a thunderstorm kicked up in the afternoon, drowning out the distant thunder of the guns along the coastline.

"One thousand one, one thousand two, one thousand three," Madame Willocque counted, sitting by the window and peering out over fields slick with rain.

"What are you doing?" Eponine asked.

Barbe gave her a look that was almost pitying. "Light travels faster than sound. By the time they have traveled a mile, light has outdistanced sound by five seconds. When I see a flash of lighting, I start counting. If I get to five, the storm is a mile away. If I get to ten, it's two miles."

"Would that the Gestapo gave us as much warning," Maman said with a snort. "All we get before they appear is a few seconds of engine noise from their Citroens."

"Enough to get the Salomon girls back to the attic," Barbe said. Eponine wasn't sure. What if they came during the thunder? Or they came on foot? She suddenly wished that they stayed in the attic all the time, as they had before she knew about them.

By Thursday Eponine gave up hope that the Allies were landing soon. The Norman weather had given up, too. The hottest, driest spell in the memory of the village's old timers had made Eponine feel as if the sky was holding its breath, waiting. Now the sky turned overcast, and the light rain so typical in Normandy started up again. Maman and Barbe knocked heavy layers of yellow mud from their shoes when they returned from planting tomatoes and lettuce. Father Simon glanced up from pulling weeds on the tumble-down stairs in front of St. Pierre's. He cast his eyes heavenward, rain dripping off the tip of his nose, then shrugged. The two SS men who usually stood sentry outside the Boivin Sisters' bread shop huddled under the overhang in front of the *epicerie*. The collars of their black coats were turned up against the damp and their heads were pulled in like sulky turtles. They didn't seem interested in Eponine, nor did they seem particularly vigilant, as if they didn't expect anything important to happen on a bleak, drizzly day.

Eponine awoke early on Sunday morning to the sound of battering rain. The windows rattled. Somewhere a loose shutter clattered cryptic morse code against the side of a house. She pulled on her bathrobe and slipped her feet into her worn slippers before she skirted the clothes horse sitting in the middle of the upstairs hall, and went downstairs. Maman, Barbe, Sarah and Ester Salomon huddled around the table. The blackout curtains remained up, throwing the room into gloom, but Maman had found some downed branches and so there was a cheery warmth from the fire and the coffeepot put out the comforting smell of roasted barley.

"No sense keeping them up there." Barbe jutted her chin toward the attic. "Not even a crazed Gestapo man would be out in weather like this."

Ester's eyes were round. "I thought the roof slates were going to fly away."

Sarah gave her sister a severe look. "Don't be rude. The Lambaols have a good, strong house."

"I was worried what the roof would do in a gale force wind, too," Maman said. She meant to be comforting, but Eponine could tell by the way Ester's face blanched that the girl found little reassurance in the words.

Eponine dashed to the cowshed and found Galopin shuddering, both from the damp and from fear. She laughed. Galopin remained calm when the bombers passed overhead. He munched grass even when the antiaircraft guns along the coast roared. How funny that he was more afraid of rain than of bombs. But then she thought, why not? Storms have been an enemy of the horse for millennia. Bombs were a new danger. She tossed a blanket over him and spoke a few words of comfort, then salved the wounds on his legs and chest. Galopin niggled uneasily. The wounds were still very tender. Eponine ran to the pasture and gathered great armfuls of grass for her old horse.

"Look at you!" Maman scowled at the puddle forming around Eponine's feet when she came back. "Soaked to the skin. Change quickly. We can't afford for you to catch cold."

Eponine ran upstairs. She slid out of her wet clothes and into a frayed woolen sweater and a flannel skirt so worn she didn't dare wear it outside the house. She wiggled her shoulders, enjoying the way the scratchy wool scoured the last moisture from her torso. Eponine hung her wet clothes on the clothes horse. She went downstairs, and found the atmosphere nearly as stormy as outside.

"Eponine got to go out," Ester whined. She was slumped in a chair, her chin planted firmly against her chest and her arms wrapped around herself.

"Eponine doesn't have to hide," Maman said. "Besides, she had to take care of Galopin. Imagine how lonely he was."

Ester pouted. "No lonelier than I am in the attic all the time."

"Stop being so fractious," Sarah said. "Pretend that you're Noah and this is the ark."

Pétain growled irritably from under the table.

"You hear that?" Maman said, looking up from the sock she was darning. "He's too deaf to hear the thunder but he's not too stupid to sense your irritation, Ester. Now stop complaining or he'll give us no peace."

"She's just bored with the weather," Barbe said.

"I assume planting is out of the question today?" Eponine asked.

Barbe snorted. "In this deluge? Let the plants fend for themselves."

"Then what if we start cutting out that new parachute fabric and make some shirts," Eponine suggested.

And that was how they passed the day, which did indeed feel like it lasted forty days and forty nights.

Eponine woke the next morning to find that the sun had come up in a clear sky. She felt a renewed sense of hope. Maybe the Allies used the storm as a screen to hide their advance. Maybe today would be the day.

She was halfway to school before she noticed the sonorous hum of airplanes and the deep bark of antiaircraft guns. These noises had become so common that Eponine, like Galopin, didn't always notice them. She realized guiltily that René, who had been gone a full week, no longer remained in the forefront of her thoughts either.

When, when, when, her heart beat.

When would the allies land?

In her last class of the day, geography, Monsieur Couturier held up a poster depicting Italy as a boot, with a snail, labeled 'the allies' crawling slowly up it. Eponine guessed by the tattered corners that he had ripped it from a wall, leaving behind four nails and some jagged pieces of paper.

"I assumed you all have seen this poster, as the Germans have recently elected to paste them all over town." He looked each child in the face, then stabbed at the German words running along the top of the poster. "You see these words right here? They pose a question. They say 'When will they reach Rome?' We finally have an answer to that, dear students. The answer is the fifth of June, 1944."

"But that's today," said Eugene, the rather dense boy who sat in the back of the room and who had taunted her on the playground with 'Eponine's an *indic*.' Eponine and the other students twittered with suppressed laughter.

Monsieur Couturier gave the blushing boy a benign smile over the top of his half-moon reading glasses. "But of course, Eugene. That is exactly what I meant."

A cheer went up, then died away. Eponine, who realized that she had thrown her hands in the air, pulled them back down and looked about. Some students had faces flushed with delight, but others looked angry and still others pale and anxious. The students in her class represented a wide range of political views. Not everyone wanted the allies to win.

René didn't. She wondered again where he was, what he was doing. Surely the Germans hadn't sent him to Rome. A wild thought raced through her head and, even though she knew it was silly, she wondered if her father had been part of the troops who liberated Rome. Maman had said that he might have gone back to the United States and joined the Army. If he was in Rome, would he come here now to continue the fight? Eponine pushed the thought away. Her mother was a hopeless romantic and a fool to believe that Papa was still alive. But her heart danced in her chest. She thought of Johannes Hegel. Was he in more danger now that Italy had fallen, or less?

"If the fighting is done in Rome, does that mean the Allies will finally land here?" Sophie Junot asked.

"Or will Hitler just give up now that his ally has fallen?" a boy added.

"All we can do is wait," Monsieur Couturier said. Eponine got a sudden, sinking feeling in the pit of her stomach. The waiting seemed unbearable. She thought of Sarah and felt a pang of guilt. Her own waiting hadn't been so bad. Oh, God, she murmured, gazing up at the ceiling, let me do one more great act before this war ends. Let me earn my freedom, and Johannes Hegel's.

And she was sure that, like Jeanne d'Arc, she heard God say yes.

CHAPTER EIGHTEEN
THE COMING STORM

Monsieur Couturier slammed his textbook onto his desk. "You are impossible! I should never have told you Rome fell. If you won't concentrate on your studies, I release you. Go home and bother your own mothers and fathers."

The classroom erupted into cheers. Chairs clattered as students scrambled to leave before the headmaster changed his mind. They had been twittering among themselves, craning their necks towards students already released by other teachers.

"Don't think I shall release you early every time you are too distracted to behave!" he shouted after them, but very few students remained to hear. Eponine flashed him a thankful smile. As she passed the music room she heard weeping. Eponine stuck her head cautiously into the room. Fraulein Mouse, the singing teacher, was hunched over her desk in the empty room.

Eponine ran home so quickly that she couldn't gasp out the news when she got there. She doubled over, struggling for air.

Maman dropped her sack of seeds and clutched Eponine. "Is something wrong?"

"Or very right?" Barbe Willocque asked.

Eponine nodded. "Rome," she managed to squeeze out.

"Rome fell?" Maman hugged Eponine even tighter.

"They can come here now," Eponine panted.

Barbe Willocque threw back her head and laughed. "Just because the Allies take Rome one day doesn't mean they take Normandy the next. These things take time. Perhaps they can start planning now that their resources are freed, but don't think they are coming tomorrow."

Eponine kept her mouth shut. She didn't dare argue with a woman who wasn't only older, but had been through concentration camp. Barbe Willocque obviously had more experience. She knew the ways of the world. Still, the same still, small voice that told her that it was wrong for the Milice to hunt down the maquisards, that her father was alive somewhere, that Johannes Hegel was honest, told Eponine that Barbe Willocque was wrong, and that the allies would come soon.. The voice of hope droned in the back of her head, incessantly insisting that things weren't as bleak as they seemed.

She was so anxious to hear The French Speak to the French on Radio Free London that Eponine nearly swallowed her dinner whole without tasting it. When it came time to go down to the coal cellar, Eponine was the first, clattering down the stairs so boisterously that Barbe had to caution her. She hopped from foot to foot while Maman pulled the radio from the rags and carefully turned the knob until the BBC came through the static. The news centered on Rome, but Eponine barely heard it. She was too focused on the messages that came after. She had no idea what she needed to listen for, but she knew that Barbe and Maman would. They finally began:

"Lull my heart with monotonous languor." A very significant look passed between Maman and Barbe. For Maman's part, the look was of knowing terror, but Barbe's face showed determined resolve.

"That means something, doesn't it?" Eponine said. Both Barbe and Maman threw up a hand to quiet her.

"The dice are on the table."

"We don't like them, we help them." Maman's hand came to her mouth to hold in her horrified gasp.

"What?" Eponine asked.

"Hush," barked Barbe.

"Those in the convent are desperate."

"The waltz makes the head whirl."

"Finally," Barbe pumped her fist in the air and then pressed it to her face to suppress a cough.

"Finally what?" Eponine asked. "What does it all mean?"

Barbe Willocque shot a look of triumph at Eponine as Maman stuffed the radio back into the tub of rags. "As you well know, none of us knows what it all means. But your mother and I do know the codes for our own little parts, and I've just heard mine.

"Which was?" Eponine bounded up the stairs after Barbe, who took them two at a time.

Barbe was halfway through pulling on her coat when she stopped and gave Eponine a piercing look. "I shouldn't tell you, but I will. I have been listening for 'The waltz makes the head whirl' for a very long time. I'm to sabotage the telephone lines between here and Reviers.

Eponine spun around and faced her mother. "And yours? What did it mean?"

"Nothing. I heard no message for me," Jacqueline Lambaol said, but Eponine knew she lied. "I'm just going out for a walk."

Eponine pushed between the women and the door. "I won't sit home alone while you go out and sabotage telephone lines."

"You aren't alone," Maman said. "You must watch the Salomons."

"Watch for what? My presence accomplishes nothing. Give me a job to do. Anything."

"There isn't anything to be done," Barbe Willocque said.

Eponine thrust her chin out defiantly. "Was there a message for Father Simon? You do remember that the Gestapo took the radio from Saint Vigor's.

Barbe's mouth dropped open. Confusion flashed across her face. "She's right," she said to Maman. She turned back to Eponine. "But I don't know what Father Simon needed to listen for. Can you remember all the messages?"

Eponine closed her eyes and concentrated. "Lull my heart with monotonous languor. The chips are on the table."

"Dice," Maman corrected. "Get it right or it may be a disaster."

"The dice are on the table. We don't like them, we help them. Those in the convent are desperate. The waltz makes the head whirl."

"Very good," Barbe said. "Check our church first. He may be there and have heard it all. But if he isn't there, check the rectory. If you still have not found him, run to Reviers. As fast as you can. We have less than forty-eight hours before they land."

Maman hugged Eponine tightly. "*Bonne chance,*" she said, then pushed her away. Eponine dashed out the door without even putting on a sweater. In the twilight she scrambled up the jumbled stone steps of St. Pierre's, tripping on an irregular step and skinning her shin. Blood trickled down her skin, but she didn't stop to look at it.

The doors of St. Pierre's were shut and locked. No light glimmered through the windows. Eponine rushed back down the stairs and through town to the rectory, which also looked dark and deserted, though Madame Tournebulle's lusty snores came from an upstairs bedroom. Eponine ran up rue de l'Eglise toward the shortcut through the fields. She was passing her own house when she heard Galopin whinnying crazily and smashing into the cowshed. Eponine feared he would rip the wall down and come right through. She dashed inside to see what was wrong.

Nothing was wrong. There was no stranger, no fox or strange dog, no snake, yet Galopin was wild-eyed and snorting, champing at the sides of the stall and pawing the ground as if determined to race.

"Hush," Eponine stared into his white-rimmed eyes. "What's gotten into you? I already took you for an evening ride. Now stay here and be quiet." Galopin reared and kicked at the wall. The image of Barbe's face, set and steely with determination flashed through Eponine's mind and suddenly Eponine realized that Galopin knew more than she had ever credited him with understanding. Galopin could tell thunder from cannons. He could sense danger. And he knew that tonight was too important to miss. Like Eponine, Galopin wanted to be a part of it.

"I can't run you, boy. Your legs are still scabbed over. But you deserve to be out here as much as I do. So, we'll walk, but walk quickly." Eponine backed her horse from his stall and slipped the bridle over his head. She slipped onto his broad back and, bending so she wouldn't strike her head on the lintel, guided him out the door.

The moment he was free of the cowshed, Galopin broke into a gallop. He raced up the rue de l'Eglise and through the fields, making for Reviers faster than he had ever gone before. Eponine leaned over Galopin's neck, holding on to his mane with both fists. His breathing came to her like thunder. His flanks heaved beneath her thighs, but she squeezed tight with her heels and let him go, hoping that he would somehow be alright. The wind whipped her hair into a froth which stung her eyes and stuck in her mouth, but she didn't dare loosen her grip to pull the strands out. Galopin didn't slow as they left the field. His hooves threw up a hailstorm of gravel. Eponine guided him to St. Vigor's and through the churchyard to the little room in the back where she had found the priest the night after the Gestapo raid had taken away Father Bertrand.

Father Simon blinked at her like an owl brought into the light, then his eyes went wide and he gasped. "What's happened to you?"

Eponine looked down. Blood streamed down Galopin's legs. A foamy, frothy mix of sweat and blood coated his chest. The blood from her shin and Galopin's legs had mixed until she couldn't tell how much of the streaky redness came from his cuts and how much from her own.

"Did you hear the BBC tonight?"

Father Simon sucked in his breath. "No. Why?"

"I will repeat the messages." Eponine closed her eyes and took a breath to help steady herself. Her shin throbbed and her heart beat so hard that she felt it in her throat. Her head felt fuzzy and distant, as if the thoughts in her head were coming from a radio just off station and blocked by German static. Maman had told her to get it right or it may be a disaster. She hoped that she was up to it. "Lull my heart with monotonous languor. The chips – no, dice -- are on the table. We don't like them, we help them.

Those in the convent are desperate. The waltz makes the head whirl."

Father Simon let out a burst of air. "I see why you rode so hard."

"We have only forty-eight hours," Eponine said.

"You've already told me that. And plenty else, besides. Now walk home very slowly and give that horse of yours the attention he deserves. But be careful; it's after curfew."

Eponine smiled. Father Simon wouldn't have to tell her twice. Eponine felt like a wrung out rag as she walked back through the dark church yard. Galopin followed. She stopped and checked his hooves for stones because he seemed lame in two legs, but the hooves were clear. Galopin's injuries wouldn't heal easily. He rested his head on her shoulder and breathed companionably in her ear, nudging it lovingly. She stroked his nose. She sensed that he, too, knew that their mission was complete. They turned out of the churchyard and ambled up the road, making for the cut in the bocage that led to the path through the fields.

All would be well now. Once the Allies landed, the Germans would retreat. The forbidden zone between her and the beaches, the ration books, hiding places in attics would be replaced by clothing and shoes, coal for the furnace, and bread and meat for the table. The men would return from POW camps and work assignments. Amblie's little shops and her school would open again. Eponine thought about the day when she would be accepted for who she now knew she was – a half French, half Irish-American girl with bravery all out of proportion to her size, who had guided downed pilots to safety, rooted out Nazi spies and spread messages for the Résistance.

Galopin heard it first. Snorting, he threw up his head in alarm. Eponine stood still. She heard it, too. The crunch of gravel under jackboots. The repetitive clink of a soldier's canteen against his belt buckle. It could only mean one thing. A patrol was coming down the road.

Eponine whirled around, looking for a way off the road. The bocage loomed up on both sides. Panicking, she considered her options. If she ran back toward the sanctuary of the church she would bring the patrol right to Father Simon's door. She could let the patrol catch her. But would they turn her over to the Gestapo for questioning? She didn't know what most of her message meant, but she did know some. The Gestapo might know the rest. She could put the entire invasion in jeopardy.

The only thing to do was make a mad dash for the break in the bocage and hope that she got out of rifle range before the patrol spotted her. Eponine threw her leg over Galopin's broad back and hauled herself up. She dug her heels into his flanks and he surged forward, ignoring his lameness. Eponine bent low over Galopin's neck and galloped directly toward the oncoming patrol. She saw them, twenty paces down the road at the same time she saw the opening in the bocage.

111

"Halt!" a voice shouted.

Frantically, Eponine pulled on the reins and Galopin veered sharply toward the cut in the hedge and freedom. They were nearly there.

A single shot rang out, then a volley. In horror Eponine felt Galopin shudder under her at the same time she heard bullets whistle past her, shredding the bushes. Galopin made a mighty leap, floundering into the bocage just short of the opening. He thrashed wildly, gaining a few feet in the thick underbrush, then stumbled and dropped. Eponine plummeted, shattering branches as she fell. Her head and shoulder slammed into the earth. Bright lights, like anti-aircraft tracers streaked across her vision.

Pain flared in her right leg and she realized that it was pinned beneath Galopin. Galopin twitched convulsively, grinding her pinned leg into the brush. He shrieked, a sound she had never heard before, which set her hair on edge. Sweat beaded her forehead and she fought the urge to scream. Pain ran up her leg like liquid fire.

Eponine heard the drone of jackboots running on the gravel road and tried to scramble to her feet, but she couldn't move. The dark hedges obscured the thin light of the new moon, making her eyes useless. She lay as still as possible, hoping they would assume that she was dead and pass by, leaving the wounded horse to his misery.

Columns of flashlight beams swayed over the bocage. They were looking for her. She held her breath and hoped the end would come swiftly and without pain.

A single voice stilled the German babble. A single beam came forward, breaking branches as he came through the hedges. Shielding her eyes from the flashlight beam, Eponine peered into the broken face of Johannes Hegel.

Sergeant Hegel bent down, his hand and light passing over Galopin's twitching, trembling flanks. He set the flashlight down and put his arms around the horse's neck, pulling so hard that he grunted with the exertion. Eponine felt the weight shift off her leg. She pulled it free and was trying to scramble away when he grabbed her shoulder and pressed her into the earth.

"I'm sorry," he whispered so quietly that Eponine barely caught the words over the horse's belabored breathing. "This isn't what I want to do, but I must. Lie very still. Be as quiet as death."

He picked up the flashlight and pulled his revolver out of its holster. Eponine could see his hand shake. She closed her eyes.

A shot rang out. Galopin ceased to struggle.

In shock, Eponine's eyes flew open. Johannes Hegel stood, his arm stiffly out, the pistol quivering in his hand.

He turned the pistol towards her.

"*Non!*" she cried.

"Hush," he murmured his voice low. Goodbye, Jeanne."

He pulled the trigger. The bullet embedded itself in the ground, a foot from her head. Sergeant Hegel holstered his pistol. He put a finger to his lips, bidding her to be silent. He called something over his shoulder, then backed through the bocage.

Eponine fell back and tried to hear over the wild beating of her own heart. The sounds of jackboots striking stones on the gravel road receded toward town. Eponine's mouth filled with bitterness. She retched until her stomach was empty, her body shaking with the effort. She wiped the back of her hand across her mouth and collapsed, staring up at the broken branches. The terror of the moment passed. Eponine scrambled up and staggered, half walking and half crawling, to a dark and seemingly empty house. But it wasn't empty, and Eponine knew it. She crawled up the stairs, her battered body protesting every inch. At the top she shoved aside the clothes rack and pressed the panel until the hidden latch popped open with a metallic ping.

"Who's there?" Sarah's voice came, strident with fear.

"Just me," Eponine climbed the ladder slowly, moving one scratched hand at a time.

Sarah gasped. "What's wrong? Are you hurt? I can't see anything in this dark."

"It's Galopin. He's," but Eponine said no more. She collapsed into her friend's arms and sobbed.

CHAPTER NINETEEN
THE STORM BREAKS

Eponine jolted awake. Someone was gripping her shoulder, shaking it. She bolted upright. Maman dropped heavily onto Sarah's creaky wooden cot. She wiped a strand of hair from her eyes. By the smoky light of the kerosene lantern Eponine saw that Maman's hair had fallen out of its twist and hung around her shoulders in disorganized clumps, bobby pins sticking out here and there but doing no good. Her face was smeared with black soot and both her blouse and her skirt was tattered.

"Thank God," Maman said in a harsh whisper. "First I couldn't find you at all. Then I find you up here, all bloody and laid out like a corpse. I thought I'd have a heart attack."

"What time is it?" Eponine sat up and looked around the low-ceilinged room. Ester slept on the other cot. Sarah, clutching the frayed, stuffed Galopin to her chest, was curled up on the floor at the foot of her sister's bed. Maman put a finger to her lips to silence Eponine, and then beckoned her down the ladder. Outside Eponine's bedroom window, planes rumbled overhead, their drone accented by the resonant boom of antiaircraft guns. Tracers and flares glowed in the southern sky like a Parisian Bastille Day celebration, but Eponine knew that either Caen or the airstrip at Carpiquet were under attack.

"Nearly midnight. God, you frightened me. Where's Galopin?"

"The Germans shot him."

Maman wordlessly gathered Eponine in her arms and rocked her. Bobby pins poked Eponine's cheeks. She shifted and her body cried out in protest. Her shin throbbed where she had fallen on the church stairs. Her back and shoulders felt bruised and scratched from the fall through the bocage. The part of her leg that had been pinned under Galopin was very tender. It would be bruised purple when she saw it in the daylight. It could have been worse, she thought. At least the bones weren't crushed. At least she was alive.

"How did your job go?" Eponine asked.

Maman chuckled. "The Germans will be very disappointed when they try to get gas at their filling depot."

Eponine straightened. "You sabotaged a gas tank?"

"*Non, ma chère.* I flirted with guards while the maquisards slipped in and set a timer."

"You could have been shot!" Eponine said.

"Could have been. Wasn't. When the tank blew to bits I slipped away in the confusion. We had a hard time, the boys and I, coming back without getting caught. I lost a clog in a muddy field." She held up a bloodied, mud covered foot, then pulled on the front of her blouse and frowned at it. "I suppose this blouse is a total ruin. Good thing we have that parachute."

Eponine giggled. "There will be clothes in the stores soon. The Allies are coming, remember?"

"They aren't bringing dresses with them. Things won't return to normal for quite some time."

"Is Barbe back?"

"No," Maman said. The grimness in her voice silenced Eponine. She shuddered, hoping that the bony scarecrow of a woman hadn't coughed at the wrong time and given herself away. She and Maman watched the firestorm outside her window for a few more minutes, then brought the Salomon girls down so that they could see it, too. Ester curled up in the blankets with Eponine. She clutched the shabby stuffed horse to her chest and oohed and aaahed as if the flashes were fireworks.

Eponine, bone tired and bruised, slipped in and out of sleep. The noise of guns and a deep sadness, like a chill that won't leave one's bones long after one has come in from the cold, permeated her dreams. Barbe might be gone forever. Eponine had never told her how much she admired her tenacity and strength. Johannes didn't know her real name. If he survived the terrible battle that he predicted was to come – if he came back after the war with his granddaughter, as he had promised, would he find her? Regret weighed Eponine down like a soaked sweater. Why hadn't she been able to convince Father Simon that her sergeant really did merit their help?

The knock on the door was faint at first, and so tentative that Eponine wasn't even sure that she really heard it over the distant thunder of war. Eponine felt her mother tense, but Jacqueline Lambaol didn't move. The daring maquisard spirit had deserted her and she was a small, worrying woman again.

"Aren't you going to open it? Perhaps it's Barbe." Eponine asked.

"I . . . I can't," Maman muttered, her hands fluttering indefinitely before her.

Eponine slid off the bed and hobbled downstairs. Her muscles ached with every movement. She squinted at the clock on the mantel. 4:30. She felt a sense of fatalism about what lay outside the door. Either she was opening it to a Gestapo squad or to Barbe. Either way, the knocking would continue until the door opened.

"Who's there?" she called, her throat tight with fear.

"It's . . . ." A hacking cough interrupted the voice. Eponine felt herself relax. She reached for the bolt. A terrible thought stopped her. What if Barbe wasn't alone? What if she had been captured by the Gestapo and forced to bring them here?

"Are you alone?" Eponine squeaked.

She heard Barbe gasp and cough a few more, strangled times. "If the Nazis were holding a gun to my head, do you think I would say yes?"

Eponine knew the answer. Barbe Willocque would die before betraying them. She slid the bolt and pulled the door open, then sagged into her house guest's embrace. The tall woman towered over her. She smelled of gunpowder and smoke, but her arms were warm and strong. "Where is everyone?"

"In my room. We've been watching the flares over Carpequiet."

Barbe chuckled. "Then you're looking the wrong way. The real show is in the north right now. You stay here while I go up and tell your mother that we're going to the well to have a better look."

"Shouldn't we bring them, too?" Eponine asked when Barbe returned.

Barbe shook her head. "Let's keep the Salomon sisters hidden until the town is firmly under Allied control."

She took Eponine by the hand and the two of them walked down the rue de l'Eglise to the beehive well. A deep red glow on the northern horizon threw the dozens of people in the crossroad into black relief. They watched silently, their faces set as grimly and noncommittally as when they had watched the Abbeville Kids attack the British bomber. Eponine couldn't tell what side the villagers were on. Perhaps they were on neither side – just waiting for German and Ally alike to leave France to herself. Eponine flinched at a brilliant yellow flash and Barbe began counting the seconds, as she did with thunder. She stopped at the count of ten, but the rumble came much later.

"I think it's Allied naval guns," Barbe whispered in Eponine's ear. "That's why we see no anti-aircraft flares, hear no engine drone. The Allies are bombarding the coastal defenses. Perhaps softening them up for a landing."

Eponine grinned. "I thought you said the landing was going to be far north of here."

"I think I was wrong. But maybe I was right and this is just a diversionary tactic."

"Pretty big diversionary tactic," Eponine said. Barbe nodded.

They walked back home, where they found Maman and the Salomon sisters cooking a breakfast of potatoes and onions bound with the single egg that Eponine had managed to get that week. The smell of roasted barley coffee filled the air.

"It's early," Maman admitted, "but I thought a celebration meal was in order. Who knows what the day may bring? Let's eat while we can."

"Good idea," Barbe said.

Sarah clinked her mug against Eponine's in a toast to the allies' arrival. "After the Allies come, we'll have real coffee."

"And chocolate," her sister added. "The Americans bring chocolate bars as big as your hand!"

"And we'll go home," Sarah said.

Maman shook her head. "Don't start packing your bags."

"Why not?" Ester wailed.

"We must make sure that all the Germans are gone before anyone knows you are here," Barbe said. "We don't want them taking you with them. Even after that, I imagine those Frenchmen who supported the Germans will try one last time to institute their policies."

"And then the infighting among the French will start," Maman added gravely.

"Maquisard against Milice?" Eponine asked.

Barbe coughed into her fist. "Nazi collaborator against Allied supporter. Things might go very badly for the Bonté family and your Fraulein Mouse."

"There will be recriminations," Maman added. "People will use the confusion in the government to right old wrongs. The Boivin Sisters have been nasty to a lot of people. No doubt someone will throw a brick or two through their windows."

"It may be months before it's safe enough to release Ester and Sarah."

"Months!" Ester wailed, but Sarah clamped a hand over her sister's mouth. Eponine kept her own mouth shut. She had been convinced that the Germans would scatter when the Allies arrived and they would be left in peace, but by dawn the thunder of war surrounded Amblie. Both the beaches to the north and Caen, to the south, were hard hit. At eight in the morning the lights flickered, dimmed, then went off entirely.

"I assume some of our own people sabotaged utilities, as we hit transport," Barbe said.

They all jumped at a particularly loud boom. To steady herself, Eponine began counting. "One thousand one, one thousand two, one thou. . . "

Barbe laughed. "You begin counting at the flash, you stop at the thunder."

Tears of frustration welled in Eponine's eyes. "I had to do something."

Maman spoke up. "Let's wait this out in the coal cellar. It's the closest thing we have to a bomb shelter." They pulled their mattresses off their beds, gathered up their blankets and pillows, and filed down the stairs behind the fireplace. Barbe helped Sarah and Ester create a mattress cave.

"But why can't we sit on the mattresses?" Ester whined. "The floor is cold and dirty."

Barbe scowled at her. "If this house takes a direct hit, you are going to be glad you had a mattress between you and all those stone walls and the slate roof."

Eponine thought of the thickness of her walls and wondered if the mattresses would do any good at all. Maman gathered the little food and water they had in the kitchen and brought it down so that they would be prepared for as long a siege as possible. Maman then got out the radio and scrolled through the frequencies. Most of the channels were broken and static filled, but eventually she found the BBC. At nine-thirty in the morning, a man named General Eisenhower came on the airwaves and addressed the people of France. Barbe translated as the General spoke:

"We must summon all our resources in order to expel the enemy from your country . . . I'm counting on your help for the crushing defeat of Hitler's Germany."

Eponine felt a rush of bewilderment and betrayal. This Eisenhower wanted her to do more? All this time, she had thought that once the Allies landed, the war would be over. Now that they were here, things were worse than ever. She pressed her lips together to avoid foolishly arguing with the General. Eponine reeled under a wave of exhaustion. She had given everything she had, even Galopin. She curled into a ball, protecting herself from the terrors of the world and, despite the rumble of war and her own despair, fell asleep.

Sarah nudged Eponine awake at five-thirty in the evening. "Listen," she whispered. "It's De Gaulle. He's going to make a speech."

Eponine wiped hard grains of sleep from the inside corners of her eyes. Her body felt beaten and sore, the scab on her shin hot and tight. When De Gaulle's voice came through, she tensed.

"For the sons of France, wherever they may be, whatever they may be, the simple, sacred duty is to fight with all the means at their disposal. It's a matter of destroying the enemy."

"No," Eponine said what she had thought while listening to Eisenhower. "I have no means left. I've lost my horse. I'm bruised, battered. There's nothing more that I can do."

Barbe Willocque smiled warmly at Eponine. She pulled her in close, enveloping her within her large frame and squeezing warmth and strength into her.

"That isn't true," she said. "There is one thing left for you to do. You shall do it as soon as the fighting dies down, perhaps tomorrow. And I think you will derive great satisfaction from it."

CHAPTER TWENTY
IDENTITY

Eponine used the shaded road to Reviers when she went on Barbe's mission the next morning. She didn't want to encounter Galopin's still form on the shortcut through the fields. Guns popped and rat-ta-tated to the north, where the Allies had taken the beaches. Blasts came from the south, where Allied bombers continued to pound Caen into oblivion. But Amblie seemed a sea of tranquility amid the whirlwind. As she passed the Mairie, Eponine noticed that the Nazi buntings and flags were gone, replaced by the French Tricolor. The Mayor, she thought, knew which way the wind blew. Eponine peered up the stairs to St. Pierre's but saw no sign of Father Simon. She passed the place where she had hidden the German spy. Was he alive or had the maquisards killed him? She shuddered. That morning, Eponine had gotten all the way to the cow shed before she remembered with a horrific jolt that Galopin wouldn't be there. She had averted her eyes from the empty stall, just as she now avoided looking at the bocage. She didn't want to think about death.

The memory of crashing through the bocage while bullets whizzed around her seemed distant, as though she had heard the story of what happened to someone else a very long time ago. Even though the scabs where the brush had punctured her shin still itched and her swollen leg throbbed, she hardly believed that she was the girl who had lain pinned under her horse until a German freed her.

Might she save Johannes, even now? Maybe she could hide the German away like the Salomons, to be peaceably handed over to the allies after tempers cooled. Eponine would talk with Father Simon after she accomplished the task that Barbe had set her to do. She walked a little faster, determined to do what she had to do before she lost her nerve.

But as soon as Eponine reached Reviers she faltered. The cobbled streets were filled with people wearing their best clothes. They were milling about cheerfully, laughing and cheering. Many, including to her surprise the school's headmaster Monsieur Courtier, carried wine bottles. She recognized her teachers Monsieur Le Doulcet and Monsieur Thibault, Monsieur Du Gouey the butcher, the green grocer and many others. The villagers crowded about two enormous green machines that looked like the German tanks with no turrets. No guns bristled from their sides. Monsieur Courtier handed his bottle over to a stranger in an unfamiliar green khaki uniform. Eponine felt a jolt of surprise as she realized how many such soldiers were in the crowd. Net-covered helmets, more bowl-like and less urn-like than German helmets, covered their heads. They carried heavy-looking backpacks, clattering an assortment of shovels, canteens and mess kits. It struck Eponine that she couldn't hear their boots. The metal studs on German jackboots rang out on the cobblestones. These soldier's black boots made no sound at all.

A solider walked up and smiled at her. "Bonjour, Mademoiselle."

Eponine's jaw dropped. "Americans speak French with quite an accent."

The man chuckled. He pointed at a flag in front of the Boivin Sisters' bakery. It was mostly red, with the Union Jack of England in the upper left corner and some kind of crest in the red field. "We aren't Americans. We are French Canadians. And it's you who have the accent."

"Oh," Eponine managed to stutter out, her mind in a whirl of confusion. "I thought the Americans and the British were coming."

"They did. The British landed there and there," he said, pointing back toward the coast, first north-west, then north-east, "and the Americans, way over there." He pointed even farther west. "But your beach and your town were liberated by Canadians."

"Oh," Eponine said again, then, as an afterthought she added "Thank you."

"You're welcome." The solider reached into a large, bulging pocket on the outside thigh of his pants. "Have a chocolate bar."

Eponine slipped it into her shopping bag. "Thank you. I will save it for a girl who lives with us."

He cocked his head. "How many children live in your house, including you?"

"Three," Eponine answered.

"Then have two more. And one for your mother. Want to see the inside of an armored personnel carrier?"

Eponine shook her head, remembering her missions. "No, thank you, but I would like to know one thing. Have you seen any redheaded soldiers?"

He looked at her curiously. "The Regina Rifles are full of 'em. You fancy a redhead for a boyfriend?"

Eponine ignored his statement. "Are any of them, well, disfigured?"

"Are they what?" He took off his helmet and scratched his head. Without the helmet he looked very Norman, with dark hair and eyes, but pale, creamy skin. He reminded her of Father Simon, but younger and less cause-worn.

"Disfigured. Burned. From the First World War."

The soldier put his helmet back on his head and smiled. "Sorry. We're all young and handsome. Not at all what you have in mind."

She went on her way, slipping through the throng, past the personnel carriers, and into the Boivins' shop.

"*Bonjour, mesdames*," Eponine called as she stepped in the door.

"Bonjour, mademoiselle." Marie and Marthe's heads popped over the top of the display case at exactly the same time. Both tiny, gaunt faces looked flushed, their movements even more jerky and birdlike. They cocked their heads to one side and peered shiftily at Eponine.

"Did you see them?" one sister squawked, patting her black hair back into its bun.

"How couldn't she? They are everywhere," the other said in her throaty crow's caw voice.

"One gave me chocolate bars," Eponine said, holding up her bag so that they could see.

"Us, too," the sisters said simultaneously.

"We made pain au chocolate out of them. Gave them out this morning," one said.

"Hooray for the liberators," the other added.

Eponine laughed. She had never seen the Boivin sisters express any sentiment besides suspicion or derision. "How kind of you!"

"Kindness, bah! They tipped in good, Canadian coin!" One jingled her apron so that Eponine could hear the coins in the pocket.

Eponine felt something akin to relief. The Germans may have gone and the Canadians come, but the world hadn't completely rolled on its axis. The Boivin sisters remained the same. She got what bread she could from them, though it wasn't her full ration, since they hadn't been able to bake in yesterday's turmoil. Her hand was on the doorknob when she turned suddenly.

"Oh, Mesdames," she said in her sweetest, most innocent voice, "has Monsieur Le Jumel been by this morning yet?"

One sister cocked her head and peered suspiciously down her long, pointed nose. "The post master? He's a late sleeper. Why do you ask?"

Eponine got out her handkerchief and mopped her brow as if very worried. "Does he come here first, before he goes to work?"

The other sister cocked her head. "Is Monsieur Le Jumel in trouble?"

"Postal workers repair telephone cables, yes?" Eponine asked.

"That is among their duties." Both sisters leaned on the case, ravenous for whatever morsel fell from Eponine's lips. She took her time, dragging out her words so they would hang on every one of them.

"And Reviers' lines were cut, like Amblie's?"

The two old biddies nodded simultaneously.

"Gossip is that whoever cut the lines also booby trapped them. If he touched a downed line, he'd be blown to bits." Eponine pursed her lips and made an explosive sound, moving her hands up to describe how the postmaster might fly through the air. She smiled and shrugged. "If you had seen him it would put my mind at rest. I guess I'll just continue worrying. Good day, mesdames."

As Eponine left she saw both sisters scramble into their sweaters. She smiled, knowing that thanks to their gossip, the telephone lines that Barbe sabotaged would stay down until firmly in Allied control. Her mission complete, Eponine strolled to Saint Vigor's Church, where she found Father Simon.

He waved a fistful of papers. "The Nazis ripped apart two hundred years of handwritten registers. However am I going to get them into their original order?"

Eponine scooped another pile off the desk and studied it. The tidy script of some long dead cleric crawled carefully across the page, recording baptisms, confirmations, marriages and deaths. The writing was difficult because she had never studied such old-fashioned script, but it was legible. "If I helped you sort through them, would you explain to me about God while we worked?"

Father Simon motioned for Eponine to sit in the desk chair. "I would tell you about God whether or not you helped me sort through this mess. That, after all, is my true job. I'm just a record keeper by default. Now, what do you want to know?"

"A great many things," Eponine said. "But for starters, would God forgive someone for being in the German army if he was really a good man?"

Father Simon leaned against the desk and studied Eponine's face. "Is this about that German soldier of yours? The one you wanted to help?"

Eponine nodded. "Do you think he survived yesterday? Is he a Canadian prisoner of war?"

Father Simon smiled. "There were no Germans in Reviers when the Regina Rifles rolled into town. They pulled out silently and quickly a few hours before."

"No Germans at all?" Eponine wasn't sure if she felt relief or disappointment. "None in hiding? None who gave themselves up without a fight?"

"None," Father Simon answered. "And no casualties or fatalities. I should know: I spent the night right here." He pointed to a cot tucked into a dark corner.

"You haven't been home since I gave you the messages two nights ago?"

"Exactly," Father Simon said.

"Madame Tournebulle's been alone? She must be terrified."

Father Simon smiled. "As deaf as she is, she probably isn't even aware that there have been bombs dropping all around her. And if she has, well, did you know that Madame Tournebulle suffers from terrible gas when she gets nervous? I may be a priest, but I'm no saint who can endure that smell without cursing. Heaven preserve her, the poor soul is better alone – and far from me. Now, tell me more about this German of yours. I think it's a story worth hearing."

She told him of every encounter she had with the German with the broken face and the big heart, how he saved her twice from another soldier's advances and once from sure death. Father Simon listened without interrupting, his face intent on hers, his hands folded and calm in his lap.

And when she finished speaking about the German, Eponine went on to speak of the other broken- faced man in her life. Although they were few and fuzzy, she spoke of every memory she had, and discovered in her own words that he, too, had a big heart that had taken in the whole world.

She talked about her isolation – how she had never known family, never even known who exactly she was or where she fit in. It seemed strange to her that, as tiny as she was, she couldn't find a tiny hole in the fabric of society to slip into, but that had always been the case. She had always been a misfit, and stranger, the only redheaded Breton in a Norman town.

"And now I know that I'm not even that." Eponine dropped her face into her hands. "How am I supposed to go on now that I have lost everything, even my identity? I'm not who or what I thought I was."

Father Simon patted her shoulder. "You will go on a new person, reborn in the truth of who you are."

Eponine looked up at Father Simon, surprised by his answer. Had he listened to anything she said? She had been living a lie her whole life, believing herself an atheist and a Breton whose father was building bridges somewhere. How could she live with truth now? She didn't know how to even begin.

"All your life you've thought you were Breton, but you were French-American," Father Simon said. "You thought your parents didn't believe in God when they were fervent Protestants. You thought you were alone and had no family and . . . . ?"

"I still have no family except Maman," Eponine said.

Father Simon shook his head. "Ask your Maman why you have never known your family. Her answers may surprise you."

"You think I do have cousins?" Eponine asked.

"Your mother went to extremes to protect you. She might have separated herself from her family to protect them as well. And as for your father's family, now that you understand how he loved the world, consider who he might have called family."

"Everyone," Eponine said. "French and Americans and Spanish."

"And Barbe Willocque and the Boivin Sisters."

Eponine wrinkled her nose. "Do I have to count those two?"

"If I must love Madame Tournebulle, then you must love Marie and Marthe Boivin." Father Simon smiled, admiring his own joke for a moment before he went on. "And another lie you've lived with is that you are tiny."

"But I am tiny," Eponine said. "There is no denying that."

He shook his head. "Jeanne D'Arc was small, yet she accomplished much. You are as large as you dare to be. You have grown quite a lot these past few weeks. It's time you realized how very big a person you are, both in bravery and in heart."

Eponine sat a little straighter in her chair. "Thank you."

She glanced at the pointed arch of the window. Light slanted down from the top point, filling the room with warmth and light. Hunger gnawed at her stomach. Could she possibly have sat there all morning? Eponine scrambled out of her chair and retrieved her market bag.

"Maman will be worried."

Father Simon stood up and stretched. "If you show me where Galopin is, I can arrange for someone to take care of him."

She shuddered, then gathered her strength together, ready to face the sorrow. "It has to be done sometime. Let that sometime be now."

They walked side by side into the noon sunshine. Father Simon took her by the elbow and she let him guide her down the street. Feeling rather child-like, Eponine tilted her head back and closed her eyes, letting the sun beat on her face. She hadn't realized how chilly it was within the sacristy of St. Vigor's, but now she welcomed the sun's warmth. Red spots danced behind her eyelids, creating patterns.

"Are they pretty, the shapes you see?" Father Simon asked.

"Very pretty," Eponine answered. "But how did you know what I was doing?"

"I could feel you weave like a blind man beneath my hand," he answered. "And I have done what you are doing many times. Flowers of the sun, I call those whorls and loops."

Eponine chuckled. "I didn't think priests did things like that."

"Priests are people too. Once upon a time this priest was a small boy who fished for minnows in the canal and skinned his knees running too fast on the cobblestones. We are at the pathway. Show me Galopin."

Eponine opened her eyes. The sun spots appeared blue in her vision, like the ones she used to imagine were Allied war ships on the Atlantic or British bombers in the air. Now, thanks to Father Simon, they were flowers. "We have gone too far. He is back here just a few . . . ." Eponine stared. The hedge was torn and battered, the branches flattened. But there was no horse.

"Someone's taken him." She could barely choke out the words.

"No." Barbe's voice came through the bocage from the field side. "Someone's buried him."

"Come see," Maman added.

Father Simon, fearing that he might rip his cassock, ran back to the path and came around, but Eponine fought her way through the broken branches until she stood opposite the three adults at a large mound of fresh dirt. She set her hand on the plank of wood that stuck out at the foot of the mound and blinked away tears.

"Who did this?" she asked.

"Come around to this side so you can see the handwriting," Father Simon said. "I think it will tell you all you need to know."

Eponine took her place between her mother and Barbe, with Father Simon behind her. She felt herself shaking as she squeezed her eyes together for strength, then looked at the wooden plank.

The words were French, but written in a formal Germanic script. "Galopin," it read, "brave horse of brave Jeanne."

"Who knew that your name was Jeanne?" Maman asked.

Eponine swallowed hard. Her heart pounded against her chest. "I have a confession to make. I'm sorry, but I had a friend, a German Sergeant. I told him that my name was Jeanne. I know it was very foolish, both to keep this friendship and to lie about my name, but I wanted a code name, just like Barbe used the name Ursule."

"It was foolish," Maman squeezed Eponine's shoulder, "and it could have gotten you into terrible trouble. But you weren't lying."

"It was a lie. I just made it up," Eponine said.

Maman shook her head. She smiled. "You must have remembered it. You are Jeanne: Jeanne Maloney, the daughter of Seamus and Hélène Maloney."

"You see?" Father Simon said. "You did know more about yourself than you knew."

Eponine stared at her mother. There was truth in her face, and a look of relief as if she had pulled off an ill-fitting mask and was finally free to breathe the air. "So you are Hélène, and I'm Jeanne. Strange, but those names don't seem strange to me. Jeanne," she repeated. "I'm Jeanne." The name sounded good on her tongue. She was going to like getting to know herself.

Eponine studied the two women. They were so different, but appearances could be deceiving. Inside, both women were determined and strong. Eponine noted how Father Simon's hand rested gently on her mother's shoulder. She remembered how his hand had gently guided her down the road. She hoped that he would guide her mother into her new life once the war was over.

"Thank you for being here for me when I found Galopin's grave," she said.

"That wasn't why we were here," Barbe said. "We were coming to tell you exciting news. Hortense has had her filly."

"Filly?" Eponine said. "It's a female?"

"And black as midnight," Maman said.

Eponine hurried back to Amblie as fast as her bruised and scratched legs would take her. Hortense ambled over to the fence, the black filly following on shaky legs. It looked so fragile, but Eponine knew that it was already strong and would grow stronger with each passing hour, each passing day. She reached out her hand and stroked the new creature between its big, glistening eyes.

"She's not yours yet."

Eponine looked up and saw René's mother standing in her doorway, her arms crossed tightly over her chest. She jerked her chin up defiantly at Eponine. "René's not dead."

"I hope she never is mine," Eponine answered. "I would rather René return safe and sound than I have this filly."

Madame Bonté's eyebrows shot up in surprise. Eponine nodded at the shocked woman, then walked back up Rue de l'Eglise. The sun felt warm on her face. Birds twittered in the trees, In the distance Eponine heard bombers pummeling Caen. Even though it seemed far away, Eponine knew that the war wasn't yet won. There was plenty still for her to do, both before the war ended and after.

The world needed to become a place of tolerance, where Jews like Sarah Salomon and red-headed strangers like Eponine Lambaol would be welcome and safe; a place of forgiveness where Johannes Hegel could return to a normal life in the country he loved and where Frenchmen on both sides of the political spectrum could work together to heal their tattered nation. This new girl, this Jeanne Maloney, had the strength and determination to see it through. Eponine Jeanne Lambaol Maloney smiled. She was going to like getting to know herself in the new life ahead.

EPILOGUE

As Maman and Barbe had predicted, the war continued longer than Eponine expected. It took the Allies until June thirtieth to break the siege at Cherbourg, a port just one hundred and eighteen kilometers from Amblie. The Germans weren't ousted from the area south of Caen that became known as the Falaise Pocket until late August. Many towns went in and out of German control. Repercussions accompanied each shift in power. In the town of Saint Amand, zealous villagers hung thirteen members of the Milice. When the Milice returned to power they reciprocated by shooting twenty six Jewish men, and later eight women and another man, and then shoving their bodies down a well. Maman and Barbe were smart to keep the Salomon girls hidden.

Many Frenchmen suffered at the hands of other Frenchmen. The first in Reviers was Mademoiselle Pithou, the music teacher called Fraulein Mouse by her students because she wore the same blue- gray skirt and sweater as German women in the military. On the afternoon after Eponine learned her real name, an angry crowd pulled Mademoiselle Pithou from her home. They stripped her out of her skirt and sweater, shaved her head and forced her to walk barefoot down the main street of town wearing only her slip. She was lucky. In other towns French women who had fraternized with German soldiers were beaten or killed.

The Bonté family didn't fare well, either. A week after Mademoiselle Pithou's humiliation, the body of Jacques Bonté was discovered in the same ditch where Eponine had found the parachute. He had a single bullet hole in his forehead. Late one night soon after, the windows in the upper floor of the Mairie were shattered with bricks. Like many of the young Frenchmen who joined *the Legion des Volontaires Francais Contre le Bolchevisme*, René was never heard from again. The Germans kept much better records of their Death Camp internees than their allied recruits. Although his name never appeared on any official registry of battlefield deaths, eyewitness reports from members of his battalion seem to indicate that he was killed fighting the Russians in the town of Koerlin in Poland on March 3, 1945. Destroyed by the loss of their sons and heckled by the townspeople they once lorded over, the mayor and his wife moved to Paris in 1946. As Hélène Maloney had in 1936, they created new histories and new names for themselves. Eponine ran into them once on a Paris boulevard, but they nervously denied who they were or that they had ever met her, and then scurried away.

Barbe Willocque, whose real name was Andrée Giraudoux, returned to teaching English literature at the Sorbonne. She never regained her shattered health and died at the age of fifty in the fall of 1956.

The man known as Moreau disappeared soon after the invasion. Although Eponine could never be sure, she believed because of the cigarettes he carried that he was an American operative who left France as soon as the allies landed.

The entire Salomon family survived the war. As evidence of how the French helped round up Jews to send to Hitler's death camps continued to mount, Sarah's father no longer felt secure in the land of his birth. In 1948 he tried to move the whole family to the new state of Israel but they were denied entry. They remained in refugee camps on Cyprus for a year, then emigrated to the United States. Sarah studied higher mathematics at the University of Chicago. Ester, who liked to argue, became a lawyer

Jacqueline and Eponine Lambaol changed their names back to Hélène and Jeanne Maloney as soon as the war was over. They moved back to Paris the following year. Hélène took a job working with the homeless and with refugees while Jeanne returned to school. A year later Father Simon left the priesthood and took a job with Hélène. The two remained good friends but they never married because Hélène never gave up hope that Jeanne's father would return.

Jeanne Maloney completed her education and became a veterinarian who specialized in the care of geriatric horses. After graduation she married a handsome young banker named Antoine Poiret. They moved to Versailles, on the outskirts of Paris, to be close to her patients yet only a short train ride from her mother and the city life Jeanne so loved. Jeanne and Antoine had four children: three girls and a boy they named René, after Antoine's father.

In 1962 Jeanne was thrilled to receive a surprise visit from a very elderly, stooped German man and his thirty-two year old granddaughter. Jeanne found Johannes Hegel just as gentle, kind and giving as he had been during the war.

How had he found her? He had stopped into a bakery in Reviers and the two white-haired old crows behind the counter had known everything about the redheaded girl who used to buy bread from them. They knew where she had moved, what her present name was, and what a success she had become. They told Johannes that they weren't surprised by her success because they had always liked that girl. Appearances can be deceiving.

ABOUT THE AUTHOR

Jennifer Bohnhoff is a middle school social studies teacher, a cross country and track coach, a volunteer with the Albuquerque chapter of Team RWB, an organization that seeks to use exercise and social activities to help veterans reintegrate into civilian life, and a soprano in her church choir.

What she loves most of all is helping people reach that "ah hah" moment when they suddenly understand the connections between themselves, the past, eternity, and the world around them. She tries to do this with music, movement, writing, teaching and simply living.

Mrs. Bohnhoff is the mother of three handsome men, the mother-in-law of two beautiful daughters and the grandmother of one very smart granddaughter with another on the way. She lives in Albuquerque, New Mexico with her husband and a petulant stinker of a cat who cares nothing for her writing.

You can learn more about Jennifer Bohnhoff and her books on her website and blog: www.jenniferbohnhoff.com

Thank you for reading this book. If you enjoyed it, won't you please take a moment to review it at your favorite online retailer?

ALSO BY JENNIFER BOHNHOFF

The Bent Reed
A Novel about Gettysburg

Available
in paperback and ebook
at your favorite online bookseller

It's June of 1863 and Sarah McCoombs feels isolated and uncomfortable when her mother pulls her from school and allows a doctor to treat her scoliosis with a cumbersome body cast. She thinks life can't get much worse, but she's wrong.

Physically and socially awkward, 15-year-old Sarah thinks her life is crumbling. She worries about her brother Micah and neighbor Martin, both serving in the Union Army. She frets over rumors that rebel forces are approaching the nearby town of Gettysburg. When the McCoombs farm becomes a battle field and then a hospital, Sarah must reach deep inside herself to find the strength to cope as she nurses wounded soldiers from both sides. Then she must find even more courage to continue to follow her dreams despite her physical disabilities and her disapproving mother.

Made in the USA
San Bernardino, CA
14 November 2014